The Rocker

That

Savors Me

Terri Anne Browning

Rock Hard & Read on

THE ROCKER THAT SAVORS ME

Copyright

The Rocker That Holds Me

Written By Terri Anne Browning

All Rights Reserved © 2013 Anna Henson

ISBN-13: 978-1491069974

ISBN-10: 149106997X

This is a work of fiction. Any characters, names, places or incidents are used solely as a fictitious nature based on the authors imagination. Any resemblance to or mention of persons, place, organizations, or other incidents are completely coincidental. No part of this book may be reproduced or transmitted in any form or by any other means without permission from the Publisher. Piracy is not a victimless crime.

THE ROCKER THAT SAVORS ME

Dedication

To my husband who makes every day a dream come true. Without you I wouldn't be able to live this wonderful dream.

THE ROCKER THAT SAVORS ME

Prologue

It felt as if I had just fallen asleep when I heard the soft, barely there tap on my window. I knew who it was and the dread felt like fists gripping my heart and stomach. Without hesitating I tossed back the worn, old comforter and moved across the small bedroom to the window. A quick glance at the clock beside my bed told me that it was just after one in the morning. I had to be up at seven to get to work—a job I only went to so that I could get Em the things she needed, like food.

Pushing back the old curtain that had been there since I was a little kid, I saw her shadow in the dark night outside. Barely tall enough to reach the window, Emmie stood on the ground in just her night gown. From the street light that illuminated the entire trailer park, I saw that she wasn't wearing shoes.

I opened the window, trying to be as quiet as I could. If my old man heard me he would come in and God only knows what would happen next. That bastard was a loose cannon at the best of times. Tonight he was drunk so I really didn't want to wake his ass up. As soon as I had the window down, I leaned out and gripped her thin little arms. She barely weighed anything!

I pulled her little body through the window and then carried her to my bed. She was shivering and no wonder. It was barely twenty degrees out, typical winter weather. Thankfully it wasn't snowing, but there was a good frost on the ground. I tucked the covers around her then moved to get a pair of my wool shocks from my dresser.

There was a scratch on her left foot, right on top. It was bleeding but I didn't dare leave my room to get her a Band-Aid. When I had her feet covered, I tucked them back under my comforter and only then did I look at her face…

Her lip was busted, blood running down her chin. Her eye was already swelling and turning an unhealthy shade of blue and dark purple. I wanted to punch something! Anything! I really wanted to just kill her monster of a mother. How dare she hurt my sweet little Emmie!

Still shivering, she offered me a pained smile. "Thanks," she whispered.

"What happened?" I whispered back.

There she sat, only nine years old, way too small and beaten. But she just gave me a shrug. "She woke me up slapping me, so I don't know. There were two men over when I went to bed. I figured she would be too busy to even think about me."

Her mother and her addictions! The booze, the drugs, and the men. Emmie had seen so much in her young life. Her house was always littered with empty liquor bottles, crack pipes, needles, naked men, and used condoms.

One day, when the guys and I made it big with our band, we were going to take Emmie away from all of that!

But for now I pulled her close and wrapped her still shivering body in my own. "Thanks for taking care of me, Jesse." She whispered around a yawn.

"I'll always take care of you, Em."

"Promise?"

"I swear it." She just gave me a smile and closed her eyes. "Always, Em." I vowed to myself when her breathing evened out and she was deep asleep. For now she was safe in my arms...

"Fuck!"

I was jerked awake hours later at the sound of my old man stomping through the house. My heart started racing when I realized that he was coming down the hall towards my room. I wasn't scared for me; he hadn't laid a hand on me since I was thirteen and I started hitting back. No, I was terrified for Emmie.

If he saw her here in my bed all bruised and bloody, he would think one of two things: I was doing unthinkable things to Emmie or I was protecting her from her mother. Either would get the cops called. My old man was a nasty bastard, which was probably why my mother had bailed when I was still too young to remember her, but strangely he had always been kind of fond of Emmie. I couldn't let him see her; I couldn't let him call the cops.

THE ROCKER THAT SAVORS ME

I knew that they would take her away. While I was all for Emmie getting out of that trailer and away from that cruel ass bitch, I also knew that the social service people would put her in a home where I couldn't protect her from all the other bad things that could happen to a pretty little girl. The guys and I had decided when we first took Emmie under our wings that she was better off where she was.

Thinking quickly, I lifted her sleeping little body and laid her on the floor. Her eyes snapped open, but I put a hand over her mouth before she could speak. "Shhh," I whispered, "get under the bed and stay quiet. Okay?"

Eyes wide, she nodded and slipped under the twin sized bed. I jumped back on the mattress and pulled the covers up to my ears. My eyes shut just as the old man opened the door to my room. "Jess!" he bellowed.

I blinked open my eyes and glared at him. "What do you want old man? I'm sleeping."

"Get your lazy ass up. Emmie girl ran off. We gotta go look for her." He turned away before he had even finished speaking.

I waited until he was down the hall before I moved. I reached for her hand and pulled her out from under my bed. Her big green eyes were frightened. "Momma's looking for me," she whispered. "She's going to be so mad."

"It's okay, Em. It's going to be okay," I promised with a smile that I hoped would reassure her. "I'm going to go out and help. You go out the window, okay?" She nodded. "Then sneak back into your room while everyone is distracted. I'll send Nik or Drake over to pretend to find you sleeping."

She swallowed hard. "She's going to beat me again."

Dread filled my stomach because I knew that was more than likely to happen, but I wasn't going to let it! "No. I got some money." I had been saving to get a new snare drum for a few months now, but this was more important. "I'll give it to her. She can get some coke or whatever. She won't care."

"Jesse…" Tears glazed her green eyes, and I wanted nothing more than to just lay there and hold my little Emmie. "Thank you."

THE ROCKER THAT SAVORS ME

The next hour passed quickly. I found Drake and Shane already outside in sweats with flashlights. The brothers looked half asleep, but there was worry in their eyes. They knew better than anyone what could happen to a pretty little girl out by herself. I gave them meaningful looks and relief seemed to wash over them.

Nik was pacing, looking more like a concerned parent than Emmie's mother who was stumbling instead of actually walking. I had grabbed my hidden stash of money before leaving my room, and while everyone was moving into groups to search for Emmie, I pulled her aside. She didn't even question me when I handed her the money. She was used to one of us sneaking her some cash to distract her from Emmie. It was all I had, but I knew that it would keep Emmie off her mind for a day or two at least. By then she wouldn't even remember this night.

"Drake, you come with me," I told him. "Shane, you and Nik go search on the east side of the trailer park."

Nik didn't even question me. He just headed off to get it done. Shane gave me a nod to let me know he would tell Nik what was going on. Drake followed me around the west side of the trailer park, and we pretended to search for Emmie for an hour. I told Drake about Emmie's lip and his face turned stormy. I knew that he wanted a drink... He was nineteen and already had a problem. I worried about him, but I think I would have worried more if he didn't have the booze to self-medicate.

Dawn was just breaking when Drake walked into Emmie's trailer and came out with her. She had cleaned up her face, and I was sure that she had even added a little of her mother's makeup to hide the growing bruise on her face. Everyone went back to their trailers, but we sat on the front steps of Emmie's. Her mother was already gone; she had taken off as soon as Drake had appeared with Emmie who had been *fast asleep* in bed the whole time.

"We can't keep doing this," Shane muttered, running his fingers through his hair. "Next time who knows what will happen."

We just sat there, knowing that what Shane said was true...

THE ROCKER THAT SAVORS ME

Chapter 1
Jesse

I woke with a start. My dreams were so real that I knew they had been a memory. Heart pounding, I sat up in my bed and ran a hand over my rough scalp. I hadn't shaved in a day or so and it showed.

It took a few minutes but I finally got my breathing under control. I had to keep telling myself that Emmie was okay. She was just down the hall sleeping cuddled up to Nik. She was safe. Her mother was dead now. No one could hurt my Emmie. I hadn't ever told anyone, but after Demon's Wings had taken off and we had started touring, I had had panic attacks every night. I had lived in a constant state of fear wondering if Emmie was alright back there in that trailer park with her mother. Thankfully, she had a cell phone, and I could call her every day—sometimes a dozen times a day—to make sure she was really okay.

Muttering a curse, I tossed back my covers and headed for my connecting bathroom. It was barely dawn but I knew I wouldn't be going back to sleep. Instead I showered, didn't bother shaving the scruff from my face or head, and went downstairs to fix a pot of coffee that could wake the dead.

After plugging in the coffeemaker, I searched the fridge for something to eat. It was pretty bare. The six bedroom Malibu beach house that Emmie picked out from the many the real estate agent had shown her was practically brand new. We moved in just a few days ago and were mostly living on takeout. The furniture wouldn't even arrive until later today.

I made myself a turkey sandwich and poured a mug full of my special brew. I couldn't survive without my coffee. I was sure that I would end up with stomach cancer one day from it, but right now I couldn't care less.

Taking my meager meal outside, I sat on the patio and watched as the waves crashed against the beach. It was soothing and the rest of my unease from my nightmare began to settle down. I sat there for a few hours loving the house that was now home.

THE ROCKER THAT SAVORS ME

It might be odd to some people, four rockers in one house, but we were more than just band mates. We were brothers, all of us. Besides, when Shane had suggested that we all needed to get our own places Emmie had lost it...

"Maybe we should get a house in the Hills. You know, me, Drake, and Jesse," Shane had said over dinner. She had told us about the beach house the real estate agent had shown her and that she wanted our opinion on the place before making an offer.

We were all in the hotel dining room, and I was trying to enjoy my steak, but I had gotten use to home cooked meals all summer and nothing else seemed to sit well these days. I saw the change in Emmie as soon as the words came out of Shane's mouth. The way she went all pale and the fear and tears that had made those pretty green eyes stick out of that gorgeous face of hers.

"Is that what you want?" she whispered.

Shane frowned. "I don't care, Emmie. I just think that since the baby will be here in a few months, you and Nik would want your own place. Having us around all the time isn't going to be easy."

Her chin trembled and I felt my heart crack open. I hated those tears! She was the only person in the world who could break me with a single tear drop. "Please don't leave me!" she whispered, but she might as well have screamed it at him from the impact it had on us all. "I...I don't want you to leave me." Her words came out on a broken sob, and I couldn't stay in my seat a second longer without holding her.

Nik's fork made a loud clattering noise as it hit his plate, and he had her in his arms rocking her before I could reach her, but I still crouched down beside of her. She buried her face in Nik's neck, sobbing brokenly while I rubbed her back. I shot Shane a glare, but when I saw his face, I looked away. He was just as broken as I was by her tears.

"Emmie, I'm sorry. I don't want to leave you. I won't, sweetheart. I swear. Please don't cry, honey." He scooted back his chair and came to crouch down beside of Nik too. He grasped her hand and tugged until she raised her head to look at him. Tears poured down her cheeks and I wanted to punch something.

THE ROCKER THAT SAVORS ME

"I don't want things to change," she sobbed. "I don't want you to leave. You guys are all I have."

Shane groaned and pulled her into his arms. Everyone around us shot us curious looks, but none of us cared. Shane dropped back into the chair beside Nik with Emmie now on his lap. He held her tight, whispering over and over again that he was sorry. That no matter what we weren't going to leave her...

It wasn't just pregnancy hormones that had caused her breakdown. The four of us were her family. All that she had ever really known. For the last six years, we had all been right there every day. I wasn't about to leave her now.

Nik dropped down beside of me sometime later. Dressed in jeans and a smoky gray Demon's Wings shirt, he looked rested and carefree. The break from the constant touring that had been our lives for longer than I could remember had been good for all of us. His carefree attitude was because of Emmie. There was only one man that I would ever trust with Emmie's heart and that was Nik.

"Gods, I love it here." Nik sighed. It seemed that like me he had gotten in the habit of saying *Gods*. Emmie's little knacks rubbed off on all of us. It was something that I didn't even notice anymore.

I nodded. "Me too."

We sat there in a comfortable silence. Nik and I didn't need to speak to communicate. We have been best friends since second grade. We knew each other's darkest secrets. I was close to Drake and Shane, but Nik and me were different...Of course that hadn't stopped me from beating his ass when I found out he had gotten Emmie pregnant. Hey, what was I to do? He respected me more for it when I was finished stomping him.

Not that Emmie knew that.

"Nik!" Emmie yelled from inside the house. The door leading out to the patio opened, and she came out with a fierce glare on her face and a phone in her hand. "You told me you weren't going into the studio until next week!"

He raised a brow at her, calm in the face of her fury. "That's right. Rich scheduled it for next Tuesday."

THE ROCKER THAT SAVORS ME

She waved the phone at him. "Then what the fuck is your producer doing calling wondering why your ass isn't already there?"

"What?" He jumped up and took the phone from her. "Look, I don't know what is going on. Rich said next week." He put the phone to his ear and walked off, speaking rapidly to whoever was on the other end of the phone.

Emmie glared at him, dropping carefully down onto the lounger beside me. I scooted over to make room. Her belly seemed to get bigger every day now. Seven months pregnant and she was nothing but stomach. It was crazy because from behind you would never know that she was carrying a load up front.

"What's going on?" I asked.

"Fucking Rich either told Nik wrong or Nik wrote it down wrong. You guys were supposed to be at the studio an hour ago. And I know that you guys will end up going in. Which means that I will be stuck here dealing with the movers. Plus I have three housekeepers coming over from Perfectly Clean for interviews." She gave me a cute little pout as she wrapped her arm around my waist.

I grimaced, knowing that she was right. Studio time was a precious commodity these days. If we wanted to get to work on our new material then we would have to go in today. I hated to leave her to deal with all of that on her own, but I also knew that she had handled worse. Fuck, she has been managing our lives for years now. Movers and a few interviews should be a piece of cake compared to that shit.

"Emmie, can you wake up Drake and Shane?" Nik came back outside. He stood as far away from my lounger as possible out of safety for himself. Emmie was bound to beat his ass if he didn't. "Jess, can you be ready in twenty minutes?"

Emmie got slowly to her feet. We had learned over the summer that standing too fast could make her dizzy. Once she was on her feet, she stormed back into the house, shooting Nik murderous glares. "I'll make it up to you, baby," he called after her. "Please don't be mad!"

"Fuck off, Nik!" she yelled over her shoulder.

THE ROCKER THAT SAVORS ME

I couldn't hide my snicker as I went into the house to put my coffee mug in the sink. From upstairs I heard her yelling at Shane then shouting at Drake to get his ass in the shower. I shook my head as I climbed the stairs to get dressed.

THE ROCKER THAT SAVORS ME

Chapter 2
Layla

I was up before the alarm went off. I already had my shower and was in the process of putting on my lipstick when it started beeping. I glared at my reflection and moved into the bedroom to turn it off. Lana and Lucy moaned and cuddled closer to each other on the bed. Both needed to get up so I could drop them off at school, Lana at the high school and Lucy at the Elementary. School had started last week, but both seemed to still be on their summer time schedule. I pulled the covers off of my sisters and clapped my hands together.

"Get up, you lazy heads." I smacked Lucy lightly on the rump. "Times a-wasting! Lana, shower. Lucy, breakfast." I left them to get up, confident that they would follow through with my commands. Ever since they came to live with me two years ago, after the death of our mother, they hadn't given me one second of trouble.

Back in the bathroom, I finished putting on my makeup and then dressed in my usual uniform of black dress pants and a white button down. Slipping my feet into a pair of flats, and I was done. With one last glance in the mirror to make sure that I was presentable, I was walking into the kitchen where Lucy was eating a pop-tart.

"Good luck today, Layla," she told me around a mouthful of pastry.

I dropped a kiss on top of her curly dark head. "Thanks, sweet pea." I had an interview today. If all went well I would have a permanent job as a housekeeper instead of just as a temporary replacement here and there. We needed this because a job here and there wasn't covering the bills. If this didn't work out I would have to go back to my old job…

Lana walked into the kitchen with a backpack over her shoulder. It weighed her slight frame down with all the heavy AP books in there, but that was the price she had to pay, and one I was willing to make her keep paying. I was determined that she was going to make something of her life. She was going to have all the

THE ROCKER THAT SAVORS ME

chances that I never had. If I was a hard ass when it came to making her study and keeping her nose clean, then that was just too bad.

"I'm ready." Lana sighed as she took a pack of pop-tarts from the cabinet and pulled a bottle of water from the fridge.

I dropped Lana off first then Lucy because it was on my way. My cellphone chirped giving me the directions that my boss, Stan, had promised me last night when he called to tell me he had put me on the list for an interview as a permanent housekeeper. The woman had asked for his three best housekeepers without a permanent position. I wasn't sure that I was one of his best, but Stan knew I needed the money.

When I got to the gate, I began to wonder who the hell these people were. When the guard asked for my driver's license and then took a moment to consult his list before making a phone call, I was really starting to worry who they might be. Who needed this kind of protection from unwanted guests? Sure this was Los Angeles County, but there were celebrities everywhere here. Whoever it was had to be someone ridiculously famous, important, or dangerous to need this kind of protection from the outside world.

After a few minutes, the burly looking guard waved me through. I followed the directions he gave me all the way to the end of the beach. When I pulled into the driveway right beside some sports car that I knew cost more than I could ever make in ten lifetimes, I nearly passed out. I was home in bed still dreaming…Right?

Behind the sports car was a little coupe that was a few years older. I figured it belonged to one of the other housekeepers interviewing. My stomach filled with butterflies and anxiety. This was too good to be true. It had to be. Whoever lived here wasn't going to hire me. They would want someone older with more experience, someone respectable.

I was only twenty five and had been working as a temporary housekeeper for Perfectly Clean for less than two years. I wasn't respectable. I tended to run my mouth, and I had more tattoos and piercings than was conventional. Most of the people I temped for made me wear long sleeves and wanted my hair kept down to cover up my tattoos. The woman who had called Stan wasn't going to want me...

Even as I thought those words, a middle aged woman with her graying hair in a sever bun came storming out of the house. She was muttering to herself and shaking her head in agitation. She got into the coupe, put it in reverse, and practically burned rubber pulling out of the driveway. I watched in horror as she nearly hit the moving van that was pulling up at the curb. The driver blew his horn at the woman, but she didn't even stop as she shifted into drive and sped off down the road.

I blinked a few times, my heart racing at the near miss that I had just witnessed. What had made her so upset?

Finally collecting myself, I stepped out of my beat-up old Corolla and started up the driveway to the front door. Behind me the driver and his crew were getting out of the van. They were laughing and cursing. I shot them a frown as I reached the door and pushed the doorbell. Moments later it opened to a woman with a full blown temper flashing in her eyes.

"What?" she snapped.

I took in the fire in her green eyes, the flare of her nostrils making the stud in her nose rise up and down with each breath she sucked in. Her auburn hair was pulled back in a ponytail and the Demon's Wings shirt she had on stretched over a noticeable baby bump. I knew who she was, of course I did. You didn't listen to the music I did and not know who Ember Jameson was. And even if you didn't listen to rock, you would know who she was if you had picked up a tabloid anytime in the last three months. The fact that she was pregnant with Nik Armstrong's baby had been big news.

This blew my mind.

"I'm Layla Daniels," I told her. "I work for Perfectly Clean and was scheduled for an interview."

She raked her gaze over me from head to toe. My long dress pants hid the tattoo on my right leg, but my shirt didn't cover the Celtic knots at my wrists, and I was sure that my shirt and bra didn't disguise the fact that both my nipples were pierced. Ember took her time on the return trip up to my face, and her head cocked

THE ROCKER THAT SAVORS ME

to the side as if she was seeing something that was particularly curious to her.

"Layla?" she questioned. "Your mother must like Eric Clapton?" I shrugged and a hint of a grin teased her lips. "Well then, *let's make the best of the situation.*"

I snorted at the line from the song and nodded. "Yeah, I never heard that one before…What did you do to that woman, by the way? She nearly took out the movers."

Ember stepped back to let me in. "Judgmental bitch! I told her that if she was hired she would have to be opened minded. I live with four rockers for the love of Gods. One of them wakes up in a pool of his own vomit more often than not. She said that it was despicable…Oh, and she wanted to know if I was sure of which one was my '*baby daddy.*'"

I bit my lip when she actually made quotation marks when she said '*baby daddy.*' I could see myself in this woman, and after only just meeting her, I felt like I had known her for years. "Wow. I would have slapped the bitch."

"Right?" She full on grinned now. "I showed real restraint." She stood holding the door open. When she heard the movers out in the driveway, she sighed. "Excuse me a minute. There was supposed to be four able bodied men assisting me today, but hey..." she shook her head, muttering about 'fucking Nik' as she walked down the few steps "...who's in charge?" she called to the movers.

A man stepped forward with a clip board in hand. His hair was short and ginger. When he smiled there was a chip in his left tooth, and his beefy hands looked more beef than hand. "Are you Miss Jameson?" He gave her a leering once over, and I felt my heckles rise. Did this fucker think they could look at her like that? I decided then and there that I was going to spend the day whether I got the job or not.

"That is me, yes." Her tone was cool, her body tense.

"Well, little lady, we got your things for you. How about showing us where you want them." His tone was full of suggestions.

THE ROCKER THAT SAVORS ME

I left the doorway and walked up beside Ember. "How about doing your fucking job instead of sexually harassing the pregnant lady, douche bag."

I actually felt some of the tension leave the other woman when she felt me beside her. "Actually, I have a better idea. How about I call your boss, tell him how you are talking to me, and see how long you keep your job."

The fucker actually had the gall to grin. "I'm the boss."

"Wow, and you are still in business?" Ember batted her eyes up at him sweetly.

"Yes ma'am. We're the best around here." I wondered why he had a southern accent if he was the best in Los Angeles County. Maybe he was the best in Alabama or Georgia from his deep drawl, although I still couldn't see him being the best anywhere with the way he was talking and practically eye fucking Ember.

"That's wonderful." She pulled her cell out of her back jeans pocket and started dialing. "You know, I heard that you guys were the best. I didn't know I would get the full pervert treatment though. I really am going to have to thank Rich for recommending you guys to me." She smiled, but I could see the steam practically coming from her ears. "Hey, Rich. How's it going you rotten pile of shit?"

"You know, I'm so thrilled with the movers that you recommended. The fact that the owner is helping with moving my things into my house is great personal service. The guys had to mysteriously had to go in to the studio a week early just hours before the movers arrived...Well, gee that was just too bad." I could hear the sarcasm, could feel the rage slowly building in her slight frame. "No, no. Thank you for all of your help...I realize you're busy, but I just wanted to let you know that Jesse will be stopping by later to beat the fuck out of you...Yes, you mother fucker! And you keep this shit up I'll have my guys signed with someone else by the end of the fucking month! I hear that bitch Gabriella's manager is just salivating to get them on board. You know, with rumors of Axton dropping you for Craig, I doubt you'd survive long without my guys."

THE ROCKER THAT SAVORS ME

There was a long pause where she had the phone pressed to her ear and seemed to be glaring off into space while she listened to whoever was on the other end. Finally she smiled a real smile this time. "That's what I thought." She pulled the phone from her ear and offered it to the mover. "He would like to speak with you."

Brows raised, the man with a slight beer belly took the phone. "Hello?" His curious look turned to one of surprise. I watched in fascination as the man turned pink, then just as quickly a sickly pale. "Yes, sir. I understand, sir. Thank you, sir."

Fingers trembling, he returned the phone. His eyes were downcast as he spoke to Ember again. "I apologize for speaking to you that way, Miss Jameson. If you would, please show us were you would like your things and we will get started… If you still want us to do the job, ma'am."

Ember's green eyes were frosty. "You're already here, so you might as well unload. I've already set up pictures of everything the way I want them placed. It's pretty explanatory, but if you have a question, ask it. Don't just assume. You fuckers aren't leaving until everything is where I want it."

"Yes, ma'am." The man nodded and turned to his men, barking orders to get started.

Ember turned to me with a grimace. "Thanks. I appreciate your help."

I shrugged. "I didn't do much, but you're welcome. If you don't mind, even if you decide that you don't want me for the job, I'd like to stay until they get done…or your guys get home."

"Let's talk inside. I could use something to drink. Would you like something?"

Chapter 3
Layla

I followed Ember into the kitchen, barely taking in the living room as we passed through it. It was empty except for the pictures on the floor showing what and how she wanted her furniture placed. She was exceptionally well organized, but I guess she needed to be after years of taking care of the members of Demon's Wings.

The kitchen had all new appliances: a huge stainless steel fridge, flattop stove, and dishwasher. There was a large island in the center with a sink and garbage disposal. Granite countertops in an earth tone went well with the yellow walls trimmed in white. There were no chairs so I leaned against the island while she extracted bottles of water from the fridge and offered me one.

"I really do appreciate your help outside. Not that I couldn't have handled it, but I've gotten a little more cautious since I've been pregnant." She rubbed a caressing hand over her swollen belly.

I nodded. "I understand. And you're welcome. That guy was such a douche, but I've come across my share."

"Trust me, in the rock business I've had my fair share too." She grimaced. "Rich is really going to pay for this one…" She muttered under her breath before taking a swallow of her water. After a moment Ember shook her head as if to shake off her thoughts. "Let's get down to business." She held out her hand. "I'm Ember Jameson…But please call me Emmie."

I shook her hand. "Nice to meet you, Emmie."

"I'm going to be straight forward with you, Layla. The first housekeeper that I interviewed this morning was nearly as bad as the second one you saw leaving. I can't relax with pretentious people like that in my house. But you, I like you. And honestly that doesn't happen often. I don't have many female friends…" she rolled her eyes "…growing up with my guys made it hard to make girl friends."

I grinned. "I'm a fan of Demon's Wings, so I think I understand what you're saying."

THE ROCKER THAT SAVORS ME

Her eyes lit up. "Awesome. I appreciate real fans. Most of the females that are fans tend to be thrill seeking whores looking for a one night stand."

I knew women like that, had grown up with a woman like that. It wasn't me. Sex with a rocker wasn't my thing. I have seen firsthand the consequences of what a one-nighter with some drunken rocker could bring. "I don't do rockers, just listen to their music," I assured her.

"Tell me about yourself." She hopped up on the counter beside the stove, swinging her legs while she studied me. "Are you married, got a boyfriend, kids?"

I shook my head. "No and no. There isn't a man in my life, and I don't want one. Men are trouble. I don't have kids, but I do have custody of my sisters. Lucy is six, and Layla will be eighteen in a few weeks."

She looked thoughtful about that for a minute then nodded. "Okay. Well, I want to offer you the job. I have to give you a three month trial period, but I really would like for you to work here."

My heart stuttered for a moment before jumping and galloping away. "Are you serious?" I asked, my voice hoarse.

"Very serious. I think we will work well together." She picked up a note pad that I had just noticed on the counter beside of her. "Let's talk benefits. I want to hire you straight out. That means that your contract will be through me and not the normal one that Perfectly Clean would require. I read over that thing they sent over and had serious issues with it." She gave a disgusted grunt. "Now, this is just the rough draft. I'll have my lawyer draft the real contract, and you can sign it at the end of the week."

"Um...okay."

"You'll have health care which includes dental. Vision is optional, but we can discuss that later. Since you have your sisters to think of we can put them on your plan. That's up to you, but don't ask my opinion on children without health care. We might come to blows over that."

"I'd like to have them both on my plan." I hastened to tell her. I couldn't have cared less if I had health insurance, but the girls needed it.

THE ROCKER THAT SAVORS ME

Emmie smiled. "Okay. But like I said, we can discuss that later." She scribbled something on her notepad. "This place is huge but we also have a guesthouse detached. It's only a one bedroom, a thousand square feet. It's completely furnished with its own kitchen, and I would like for you to move into it. I'm sorry but I need a live in. We don't have parties or anything, but my guys need cleaning up after, more on an hourly basis than a daily."

Was she for real? She wanted me to move in? I couldn't answer her I was so shocked. She frowned at my continued silence. "I understand if you don't want to, what with your sisters. I mean these are rockers, and they have lived a hard life. I wouldn't want my sisters subjected to that either, but..."

"No!" I shook my head. "No, that isn't it. I don't care to move in." Fuck, I was a month behind on my rent and had been expecting my shrew of a landlady to knock on my door any day now with an eviction notice. I was sure that I was dreaming, or I had stepped into some alternate universe where everything went my way. "And Lucy... She's seen worse."

Emmie's green eyes darkened. "Worse?"

I gritted my teeth, thinking about the life that my baby sister had to live until the death of our mother. I hadn't even known that Lucy existed until I got a call from social services two years ago. "My mother wasn't the best mom."

She looked away, her jaw tense. "Yeah, okay. I understand that." Her throat worked and she was quiet for a long moment. When she looked back at me, her eyes were glassy. "The bedroom has a king sized bed, and the sofa in the living room is a hide-a-bed. Will you move in?"

"Yes. I can do that."

"Good..." More scribbling on the pad. "Before we talk numbers I want to tell you what I expect."

"Fair enough."

"I want the downstairs to be your main priority. My office is in the back of the house, but I'll take care of that. Please don't go in there unless you talk to me first. The guys can take care of their rooms for the most part, but laundry is a hopeless chore for them.

THE ROCKER THAT SAVORS ME

They will bring you their baskets when they need it done. I want the bedrooms vacuumed weekly. The toilets also, with the exception of one room. I need that one done every other day. I'll show you."

All of her expectation sounded reasonable. Emmie wanted me to cook breakfast and sometimes put lunch together. I was responsible for the grocery shopping, and there would be a list of needs/wants. "Please. When you shop for this house, be sure to stock your own fridge while you are at it. Don't you dare let me find out that you are paying for groceries out of your own pocket! That is unacceptable."

"I..." How did I respond to that? I didn't like taking handouts, but this woman didn't make it sound like it was. "Okay."

She smiled. "Good. Don't ever argue with me on that. I'd hate to have to fire you because of it."

I held up my hands in surrender. "I swear I will not argue with you on that."

She cocked her head to the side like she had when we first met. "But that doesn't mean we won't argue?" I shrugged and she laughed. "Good. I don't want some meek little mouse scared of standing up to me."

"Don't worry. I'm nowhere close to meek."

She was scribbling again on her notepad, and then she tore off a corner of the page and offered it to me. "This is a weekly number. If, after the first week, you decide that it isn't enough...and really, I kind of expect that to happen, so don't be afraid to come to me and talk about it...we can revisit the numbers."

I didn't take the paper at first. I was curious as to why she would say that. "Why would I think that you aren't paying me enough?" Fuck, she was providing me a place to live and food in my fridge. All my personal needs met.

She sighed. "Drake's bathroom...Well, just promise me that you will come to me if it gets to be too much, okay?" She waved her hand at me. "Please, take it."

I finally took the piece of paper from her and glanced down at the number written across it. That was when I was positive that I

THE ROCKER THAT SAVORS ME

was still home in bed. Fuck! I hadn't made that kind of money in a month at my old job. And she wanted to pay me that a week? What kind of mess did Drake make if she was willing to pay me more?

"Do you accept?"

"I…I…" I clenched my jaw to stop the flow of stammering. Sucking in a deep breath I nodded. "I accept."

THE ROCKER THAT SAVORS ME

Chapter 4
Jesse

My head was killing me by the time we got back to the house. I had spent the day pounding out the same song over and over on the drums to the point that my ears were ringing with the beat. I wanted a handful of ibuprofen and a shot of Patron with a desperation I knew Drake felt too.

Shane pulled the Escalade into the driveway beside of a beaten up gray Corolla. The thing looked like a death trap, but I wasn't going to judge. My first car had the entire passenger floor boarding missing. I just hoped whoever Emmie had hired to help her out around the house had gone shopping because I wanted food that didn't come out of a carton tonight.

I was the last one to enter the house. Drake took off straight for his room, probably to find one of his Jack Daniels bottles. Shane muttered something about a run to clear his head, and Nik was already yelling for Emmie. "Where are you?" he called out.

"Back here in the office." I heard her yell back.

I took my time. The movers had done a good job setting all the furniture up that Emmie had chosen. The living room looked comfortable, cozy even. The long, dark brown sectional faced the big screen hanging in the corner and the wall of glass that looked out onto the beach. I figured I wouldn't be watching much television with that view to distract me. End tables with red lamps on them sat at each end of the sectional with a round, glass coffee table in front of it. The walls were bare, but Emmie wanted to hang up Demon's Wings posters and all our awards over the years. She had probably been too busy to even care about the walls today.

I heard Emmie laughing and then someone else joined in. The beat from today's song finally seemed to clear from my ears at the sound of that laugh. It was all husky and teased me with its sexiness. Without even realizing it, I started down the hall towards Emmie's office. I had to see what went with that laugh.

Nik was standing in the doorway when I reached the office. Emmie was saying something, apologizing I think. It would have been something I would have gotten my phone out to record if I wasn't so intent on finding the bearer of that sexy laugh. Nik stood in my way, blocking my view of whoever was setting in front of the desk.

"I guess Rich is still blaming me for you guys canceling the winter tour, so, I'm sorry for being a bitch this morning when you had to go into the studio. It wasn't your fault."

"I don't know what to say." Nik shook his head. "I'm speechless."

"That Rich would do something like that?"

"No. That you would actually admit that it wasn't my fault…" He suddenly ducked and I was taken by surprise when a half empty bottle of water smacked me in the chest.

I grunted. "Good arm, Em." I bent to pick up the bottle then pushed Nik out of my way so I could enter the room.

I wasn't expecting the woman sitting in the chair. In fact, I was so surprised I nearly stumbled at the sight of her. Her laugh had deceived me. That sexy laugh had absolutely nothing on the goddess sitting there with her long cinnamon hair flowing around her shoulders and those big chocolate eyes that melted me when they met mine. Even sitting down, I knew she wasn't tall, maybe five and a half feet. Her white button down top was just a little snug across her breasts that I instantly wanted to taste.

My reaction to her stunned me. I had never gotten hard like this. Even after a show, I was more jacked up on the adrenaline of playing for a hyped up crowd than the actual need to get between a woman's legs. Right now, I was hard as a rock after only a few seconds in her presence.

"Jesse, this is our housekeeper, Layla Daniels." Emmie introduced us. "Layla, this is Jesse Thornton."

She stood and offered me her hand. I towered over her but that didn't seem to intimidate her. I even got a grin. God, that grin! "It's a pleasure to meet you, Jesse."

My hand swallowed hers when I took it. Her skin was soft and warm, and I felt an electrical current zap through my blood straight to my dick at the first touch. "The pleasure is all mine, Layla," I assured her. God damn, she was so beautiful.

Would Emmie kick my ass if I seduced this little goddess?

THE ROCKER THAT SAVORS ME

My gut told me yes, but my dick said that it didn't care.

Those chocolate eyes darkened to black, and I saw her nostrils flare ever so slightly. I had seen that same reaction millions of times from an endless supply of women. Layla was just as affected as I was. That thrilled me. The next moment she pulled her hand away and turned back to Emmie. "It's getting late. The girls are probably wondering what happened to me."

"Okay. I'll see you first thing in the morning then..." Emmie stood "...thanks for all of your help today, Layla. I could have gotten it done without you, but I'm so glad that I didn't have to."

Layla grinned. "It was fun. See you tomorrow."

I actually turned to follow her out, but Emmie grabbed my arm and held me back as Layla made her exit. When she was safely out of sight I frowned down at the pregnant woman holding on to me. "What?"

Her eyes were both amused and serious. It was an odd combination. "Please, don't fuck the housekeeper. I like her and if you do something that makes her quit, I will break your favorite drum sticks." I glared down at her. She knew how to fight dirty. "I mean it, Jesse. No playing around with her. She's not like the girls you are used to."

Fuck, I knew that. One look at her and I knew that she wasn't going to be like the women from my past. I wanted more than just one night with that little goddess.

"Jesse…" She punched me in the arm. "Please?"

I blew out a frustrated sigh. "I can't promise," I told her honestly. I would never lie to Emmie. Never. "I…want her."

Layla

The rest of the day seemed to go by quickly after my initial shock wore off. I helped Emmie instruct the movers while she divided her time between the men and answering her cell phone. I realized early that she was a little ball of energy and was left wondering where she got all that from, especially as pregnant as she was.

Once the furniture was the way Emmie wanted it the movers left, I was given a shopping list half a mile long. "I'm sorry to put this on you today, but the fridge is bare and we are all sick of eating out of boxes." She sighed. "Do you know how hard it is to get good Chinese with bacon on it?"

"Umm... No, not really." Bacon? What?

Emmie laughed at my wide eyes. "It's a pregnancy thing. I have to have bacon on everything or I'm not happy. And if I'm not happy, this little girl isn't happy." She rubbed her hands lovingly over her bump, something I had noticed her doing a lot of today. "So it's bacon or nothing."

I noticed on the list that bacon was underlined a half dozen times with exclamation points. The number six was next to it. "Is this a weekly shopping list?"

"Yep." She handed me a credit card that had her name on it. "I've already alerted the right people that you will be using my card occasionally. Just sign your name and bring me back the receipt."

It took me two hours to get the shopping done. When I returned to the beach house, Emmie was in her office with the door shut. As I unloaded my car and put away the groceries, I heard her voice rise every so often as she yelled at whoever was on the other end of the conversation.

It was just after six before she came out and asked me if I would make her a sandwich. She looked tense and I hadn't seen her eat anything all day. Concerned, I pulled out the fixings for a turkey sandwich. "Go sit down, Emmie. You look beat. I'll bring the sandwich to you. What would you like to drink?"

She sighed tiredly, her supply of energy having been depleted for the moment. "I don't care," she mumbled and went back towards her office.

I quickly put together a sandwich with lettuce, tomato, cheese, and a little mayo. I put a pickle on the side and because she had said that she had to have bacon, I wrapped a few slices of the microwaveable bacon in a paper towel and nuked it before putting it on her sandwich too. A bag of pretzels and a glass of milk, and Emmie's snack was ready. I found a tray and carried it into her.

THE ROCKER THAT SAVORS ME

She was leaning back in her chair, eyes closed, when I walked in. "When was the last time you had anything to eat?" I asked as she took a small bite of the sandwich.

"I had some toast this morning." She grimaced. "I know, I know. I need to take better care of myself. Trust me, baby girl here is making her displeasure known."

"Can I get you anything else?"

"You can fix yourself a sandwich and join me. I hate eating alone." She took a larger bite of the sandwich. "And maybe another one of these bad boys."

I grinned. "You got it, boss."

For the next twenty minutes we chatted and ate. I hadn't realized I was hungry until I sat down and took the first bite of my sandwich. Emmie inhaled her first one before I returned with the second one. By the time we had swallowed our last bites, I felt like we had begun to develop a kind of friendship.

I took our dishes back to the kitchen and put them in the dishwasher, but Emmie called me back no sooner than I had the door to it closed. "Come keep me company," she called out.

I had barely taken my seat when I heard the front door open and what sounded like a herd of buffalo storm into the house. Emmie's eye lit up. "My guys are home."

The way her green eyes sparkled told me that she loved them all. I wondered about story behind them but kept my curiosity to myself. Someone called out for Emmie from somewhere, and I watched in complete fascination as those sparkling eyes darkened with something like passion. "Back in the office," she called back. "Crap, I'm going to catch hell. I have to apologize for this morning."

"Not something you do often?"

Emmie laughed. "I don't like to give them that satisfaction."

I couldn't help but return her laugh just as the door was filled up with the delicious sexiness of Nikolas Armstrong. "What's so funny?" His voice was just as sexy as when he sang.

"I'm sorry," Emmie blurted out.

Nik looked stunned. "About?"

She grimaced and told him about our day. Apparently, it hadn't been Nik's fault that he had to go into the studio this morning after all. Rich told him wrong, knowing that Emmie would be stuck with the movers on her own. Pay back for Demon's Wings canceling their winter tour.

"I don't know what to say." Nik shook his head. "I'm speechless."

"That Rich would do something like that?"

"No. That you would actually admit that it wasn't my fault…" Emmie picked up her half full bottle of water and threw it at him with a precise aim that impressed the hell out of me. Nik had the good sense to duck.

The bottle hit the chest of pure male perfection behind Nik which caused the man to grunt. "Good arm, Em." He bent to retrieve the bottle before pushing past Nik who was snickering.

Okay, I have to admit that I have always considered every member of Demon's Wings sexy as hell, but I'm a freak for bald guys. Even with the little bit of scruff on his normally smooth head, which told me what I had always wondered about—did he shave it like that because he had to or because he wanted too? Answer? Because he wanted too!

My reaction to him surprised me. If I saw a bald guy I was usually interested enough to take a second look. Something about him when those brown eyes caught mine and he shook my hand, the way that I felt like I was struck with lightning at just that innocent touch, and I was ready and willing for him right then and there! Then I remembered who he was and pulled away. Rockers were bad news. I knew that because my mother had had a thing for them. I was the result of her first journey into the world of hard rock and roll. Just as both my sisters were her continued need to be a rocker's plaything. Rockers spelled trouble in my book, and I was not going to go down that road no matter how wet my panties suddenly were, dammit!

I made an excuse to Emmie and got the fuck out of there. All the way home, I kept telling myself that I would have to stay away from Jesse Thornton.

THE ROCKER THAT SAVORS ME

I used my key to unlock the apartment door and was almost trampled when I walked through the front door. The first thing I was going to do with my first paycheck was get us all new cellphones so we could stay in touch. Lucy was pale and Lana had a scowl on her beautiful face. I instantly felt guilty for having worried them. It was after eight, but I had always been home by six, even on my most busy of days.

"Where have you been?" Lana demanded, sounding more like a mother than our own mother ever had. She had taken care of Lucy for the first four years of the little girl's life, so she was used to worrying about someone other than herself. Lana was strong and extremely mature for someone so young.

I pulled the bag of greasy hamburgers from behind my back and offered it to her as a peace offering. "I come baring food and good news."

"You got the job?" Lucy was already jumping up and down with excitement.

"I got the job," I told her, hugging her close and dropping a kiss on top of her sweet smelling hair. Lana must have already helped her with her bath. "Let's sit down and talk. I have some news."

We sat down at the little scarred up kitchen table, and I handed out the burgers that I knew they loved but hadn't been able to afford often. There was a saucepan with mac and cheese on the stove, so I knew they had already eaten, but the girls would never turn down grease and saturated fat.

I was going to miss this apartment. It had kept me safe and warm for the last five years. I liked its warn wallpaper and the dull, egg color paint on the walls. It was small, only a one bedroom, and barely housed three females. The girls took the bedroom while I slept on the worn, old sofa that I had inherited from the tenant before me.

I waited until they had inhaled the first half of their burgers before telling them about my day. I wiped my mouth and fingers on a napkin and took a sip of my bottled water. "So…I got the job, but they are hiring me straight out instead of through Stan."

Lana's brows rose. "Is that good or bad?"

THE ROCKER THAT SAVORS ME

I grinned. "It's good. It's really good, Lana," I assured her. "We're getting health insurance, and they are paying me triple what I would make working through Stan for a month…in a week." Lana's eyes got huge and I nodded. "So it's a good deal."

"Where will you be working?" she asked around a mouth full of beef, cheese and veggies.

"Malibu." I didn't know how she was going to react when I told her about us moving, but I had to do it now. "My boss has a guesthouse and she wants me to move into it, so I will be on call twenty-four seven. She knows that I have you girls to take care of, and she said that it was okay."

Lana nearly choked on the food in her mouth when she swallowed too quickly. I pounded her on the back a few times to help her catch her breath. Her eyes were watering but she was able to wheeze out a strangled, "What?!"

"Does that mean we're moving?" Lucy asked, her little brow puckered.

I nodded. "Yes, Lucy. We are moving and our new place is right beside of the beach."

She clapped her hands together. "That's so cool!"

"But we can't move!" Lana objected. "I mean that's awesome and all, Layla. Really. It's the beach, who wouldn't want that? But I can't transfer now."

"You won't have to. Lucy is going to have to change schools, but you won't. You can use my car and drive to school. I won't need it." If her eyes got any wider, I was sure they were going to pop out of her pretty head. I hadn't even told her the biggest news yet!

"I don't care if I change schools," Lucy informed me around a mouthful of cow, pickles, and ketchup.

"I'm glad, Lucy. I really think this is going to be a good thing for all three of us." I took another drink of my water. "I just need you girls to do one thing for me, okay?"

"What?" Lana questioned, still sounding a little strangled. I knew how she felt. Today had been one big surprise after another for me too.

THE ROCKER THAT SAVORS ME

"Well, the people I'm going to be working for are really famous. They need their privacy. We can't talk about them to anyone. So if anyone asks you who I work for, you tell them you don't know. And you can't bring friends over."

Lana laughed at that. "I don't have time for friends anyway, Layla. So that isn't going to be a problem." I was a hard ass about studying, but she wanted a good education just as much as I wanted it for her.

"What's your boss's name?" Lucy asked.

"Well, the woman who hired me is called Emmie. She's my boss..." I met Lana's eyes and grinned "...but the guys that live there are in a band called Demon's Wings."

"No way!" Lana exclaimed. "No way!" She wasn't a big fan of the rock genre like I was, but she knew exactly who I was talking about.

I laughed. "Yes way!"

"They're demons?" Lucy asked with fright in her dark eyes. "I don't think I want to live there, Layla."

"Oh, Lucy, baby no. They aren't demons," I quickly assured her. "That's just their name, honey. I promise you, they aren't demons."

Chapter 5
Layla

I found out why Emmie was willing to offer me more money the next afternoon.

By the time I got to the house in Malibu, the band was already gone. More time in the studio, Emmie told me. I was glad that I wouldn't have to worry about running into Jesse. After a night filled of some really naughty dreams about the sexy drummer, I wasn't sure I could look him in the eye and not jump on him. That wasn't a good thing. Emmie would probably fire me on the spot for attacking the man.

For the first part of the morning, I helped Emmie hang pictures. Mostly they were beautifully framed posters of the band. A few had Emmie in them. I'd had seen several of them over the years. I really liked the one with Emmie pressed up against Jesse. She was wearing a pair of jeans and nothing else. Her auburn hair hung free and her breasts were pressed against his side. It didn't come off trashy like some I had seen in the past were the girl was all skanky. The other guys were all shirtless as well, with the brothers on either side of Jesse, and Nik glaring into the camera from his position just behind them, as if daring the world to say anything.

I helped decorate the living room with things I had never even dreamed of touching before in my life: Grammys, MTV video awards, platinum records. I was scared to touch some of the awards that Emmie had carefully wrapped in a box, like the crystal guitar that the band received in London for *Rocker of the Year* just the year before. It was beautiful and I was terrified that I would break it.

After a small lunch that Emmie insisted I share with her in her office, I got to work on the upstairs. I vacuumed and scrubbed the toilets. I even picked up a few dirty clothes and put them in hampers. It was easy to decipher what bedroom belonged to whom. The bass guitar in one told me it was Shane's. The drumsticks on the bedside table on another assured me it was Jesse's. When I got to the bedroom at the end of the hall, I knew that I was in for a treat. I didn't need to see the Gibson and Fender guitars against the wall of this bedroom to realize it belonged to Drake.

I smelled it as soon as I opened the door. It was unmistakable, that stench that comes with vomit and sweat, but I had a very strong stomach. It took me an hour to get the smell out. I opened the window in the bedroom and the one in the bathroom. I scrubbed every surface in that bathroom with bleach and then went back over it with two other cleaners. I smelled like the chemicals I had used, but at least the bathroom no longer smelled like the men's room at the club I use to work at.

I put away my supplies in the laundry room before going in search of Emmie. I needed to talk to her about that room. When I found her she was glaring at the screen on her laptop with her cellphone pressed to her ear. "I said no. You know how I feel about her. I don't really give a fuck. Who cares?" She raised her head when I knocked quietly on the office door. "Ax, I have to go."

She tossed the phone aside and motioned me in. As I walked closer her nose wrinkled. "You smell like a bleach factory."

"Sorry. I just finished cleaning the bathrooms... Listen I need to talk to you about something."

Her eyes darkened. "I told you it was going to be bad, Layla. Just tell me how much more you want."

I stopped, taken aback. "No. No, that isn't what I wanted to talk about." She frowned but didn't say anything so I went on. "You said that you wanted his bathroom done every other day, but I think it would be better on us all if I can get in there every day."

"Oh." She seemed surprised. "So you aren't demanding more money?"

"No, of course not. I've cleaned worse things than that bathroom." Much, much worse. "So is it okay?"

"If that's what you think is best."

I nodded. "It is... And is it okay if I change his sheets every day too?"

"Layla, I hired you to help me out around here. That doesn't mean that you have to worry about Drake to that extent." She didn't sound irritated, just concerned for me. "I don't want to overwork you."

"Please?" I didn't think I could stand the thought of Drake having to sleep on those sheets every night. They had been tossed every which way and the stench of sweat and fear had been worse than the actual smell of the vomit.

"I…" She was still frowning at me, but she nodded. "Okay. If it means that much, then you have free rein in Drake's room. Clean what you think needs cleaning."

"Thank you." Her phone rang and I turned to go so that she could get back to doing whatever it was that she did.

"Layla?" she called after me as I started to close the door.

I stopped and looked back at her. "Yes?"

"Thank you. Drake is special…and he needs a little more TLC than the rest of them sometimes." Her voice was choked and she blinked several times to keep the tears in her green eyes from falling. "So thank you."

Before I could answer she picked up her phone. "I told you that I don't want to have dinner with you and the bitch troll, Axton."

I changed Drake's sheets and pillow cases and put his comforter in the heavy duty washer. By the time I was done, his room smelled so much better. I didn't understand what Emmie had meant by him being special, but I was glad that I could make him feel like he was.

It was almost six before I told Emmie that I was leaving. She was in the living room with a bowl of cereal. "Okay, thanks. Oh, tomorrow I want to show you the guesthouse. I meant to do it today but things got away from me. Have you talked to your sisters about it?"

"Yeah, they seem excited. Lana was worried about changing schools, but I assured her that she could use my car so that she wouldn't have to."

"I wouldn't want to leave my friends either." She put her empty bowl on the glass coffee table.

"That's not it. I think she could care less about all of that. Mostly she was worried about all the extra classes she's taking."

THE ROCKER THAT SAVORS ME

Emmie patted the sectional beside of her, and I dropped down on the edge. "She's crazy smart, and I push her hard. She already has enough college credits from all the extra AP classes to start college as a sophomore. Her education is important to us both."

"Wow. She sounds like a good girl."

"She is. Lana has her head on straight." I was proud of that girl. Even after all the shit our mother put her through she was still so strong and loving.

"Well, I can't wait to meet her." The front door opened without warning and in walked the band. She stood to greet them. "Hey!"

"Emmie, I'm starving." Shane dropped a kiss on her cheek. "Tell me you made something that doesn't have bacon on it."

"I thought we could grill out on the patio. Burgers and hotdogs okay?"

"As long as it isn't from a fast food place, that's perfect." He rubbed his hand over her distended belly lovingly before focusing on me. "Well hello there, beautiful."

I couldn't help but grin. I knew all about the reputation of Shane Stevenson. There didn't come a bigger horn dog. This man was king of orgies, or so the trash magazines had said. "Hello."

Emmie muttered something under her breath and shook her head. "Layla, since you are a fan I'm sure you know who this is. Shane, this is our housekeeper, Layla Daniels. Our *housekeeper*, Shane. And her job does not include personal turn down services."

He looked a little disappointed but still offered me his hand. "I love your name, Layla. I'm a huge Clapton fan."

"You're a huge something," a deep voice informed him, and my heart actually skipped a beat. Jesse shoved Shane from behind. "I thought you wanted a run."

"I changed my mind." Shane gave me a wink. "Excuse me, Layla. It was a pleasure to meet you."

I watched him go because it was safer to look at Shane than at the hulking piece of male perfection standing mere feet from me. "It was nice to meet you, Shane," I called after him.

"Baby, I missed you." Nik came into the living room looking tired. I guess working on their new songs was hard work. He pulled Emmie close and kissed her softly on the lips. It was sweet and yet none the less passionate. I had to avert my eyes because the look on Emmie's face was so full of emotions.

Jesse grunted. "Break it up, you two. I can only stand so much of that before I want to break Nik's face."

Nik shot him the finger without even lifting his head. I grinned and picked my keys up off the end table where I had left them earlier. "Well on that note I think that I will head out."

"You can't leave. We're going to cook out." Jesse followed me out of the living room and stood in front of the door, blocking my exit. "I grill a mean cow." He gave me that cocky grin that had literally melted my panties yesterday. "Come on, Layla. Don't go home yet."

I was so tempted. I wanted to stay and not just to try out his mad skills with the grill on the patio. My heart was aching to be close to him just as much as my body was. That alone terrified the shit out of me. "Maybe another time. I really have to get home." Wait, why did I have to get home? Oh yeah, the girls.

His eyes narrowed. Was it me or had his eyes actually changed color? That was so sexy! "Do you have someone waiting for you?"

"Yes," I told him honestly. His eyes darkened and for some reason I was quick to tell him about the girls. "My sisters."

Those incredible eyes of his changed again, turning back to the brown from earlier. "Sisters?"

I grinned. "Yes. I have custody of both my sisters. They will be wondering where I am, so I really have to get home."

"Call them and ask them to join us. Tell them to grab a cab, and I'll pay the driver when he gets here." He took a step closer to me, and my breath caught in my chest. "You know you want to stay," he whispered.

I tried to keep calm, tried to remember how to breathe, but he was too close, too alluring and smelled to damn good. "I…" I had forgotten how to form words.

"Call them."

Finally, I found the strength to suck in a deep breath. "I can't." I couldn't let Lana and Lucy ride in a cab by themselves all the way out to Malibu, especially when they had school in the morning. The disappointment in his eyes—*oh goodness, they've changed color again*—made my heart ache a little. "They have school in the morning," I told him. "I would love to stay, really, but school is important."

His mouth lifted in half a smile. "Okay, I understand." He stepped back enough that I was able to breathe without getting assaulted with that deliciously sexy smell of his. It wasn't cologne, but something both subtle and hypnotizing. "Drive safely."

Jesse opened the door for me, and I was reluctant to walk out. I had to force my feet to move. The entire drive home I felt almost depressed.

Stupid, stupid, stupid! I was already developing feelings for the rocker.

Jesse

It was crazy but I felt depressed after I watched Layla pull out of the driveway in her beat up old car. I had been thinking about her all day, had woken up hard as a fucking rock twice the night before with her on my mind.

I hadn't wanted to go into the studio this morning because I wanted to see her again. Then when we got home it was to find Shane undressing her with his eyes and her grinning up at him like she knew it too, so I might have shoved him a little harder than was deemed playful to get him to keep his eyes to himself.

Layla Daniels had invaded my mind, and I didn't know why, but I was willing to explore the possible answers. I wanted her with an ache that I had never felt before in my life, but it was more than that. I wanted to get to know her too, and that wasn't me. Jesse Thornton didn't care about getting to know women. All he cared about was his band brothers and Emmie. I was a bastard like that, but they were all I knew and all I loved. Nothing else mattered.

Yet here I sat with this desire to know that little goddess inside and out. Sisters? Why did she have custody of them? How old where they? Did they look like her? Where were her parents? I wanted to call her to ask her all of those questions and more, a million more. I had never called a girl in my fucking life!

"You're quiet tonight," Emmie commented around a mouthful of the bacon cheeseburger I had made for her. I was getting tired of the very smell of bacon, but that was all she wanted, so that was what she'd get, even if I gagged at the thought of eating another slice of pork again.

"He's been moody all day," Shane muttered, taking a swallow of his Corona.

Emmie gave me a long thoughtful appraisal. She knew us all inside out, so I knew she would realize what was wrong with me. I wanted to talk to her about it and hated her for seeing so much. "You really like her, huh?"

I shrugged, not wanting to talk about it with the other guys sitting right there with us. Nik's head shot up from playing with something on his phone. "Who?"

The brothers seemed just as curious. I raked a hand over my smooth head and glared up at the star filled sky. "Okay, so I like her. She's..." I broke off because I didn't know what she was like. I was attracted to her on a deeper level more than any other woman I had ever met, and from the few minutes I actually spoke with her, I had enjoyed her personality.

"She's great," Emmie told me. "She's sweet and caring. I love that she can get just as bitchy as I can. I don't have to ask her to help me because she jumps right in without complaint. I could really see her as my friend."

We were all surprised at Emmie's praise of the other woman. Emmie had a hard time trusting other females. Her monster of a mother had really fucked her up and she felt like she could only trust herself. The guys and I hadn't helped much in that department, letting her see how other women acted around us and subjecting her to all the jealous bitches that wanted to be her simply because she was the only female that would ever hold our hearts. If Emmie thought that Layla was already good friend material, then there was something very special about Layla indeed.

"So…" Shane took another pull from his beer "…Jesse likes Layla. She's so fucking hot, dude."

Emmie, seated between him and Nik, smacked him on the back of the head. "Respect, Shane. Respect."

"What?" He grinned at her. "She is. Come on, Em. Tell me you don't think she's hot. Tell me."

"She's beautiful," Emmie conceded, "but you guys need to show her some respect. I mean it. You will not talk to her like you do your little sluts. And with her and her sisters moving in this weekend, you will clean up your language. Understand?"

"She's moving in?" That news blew me away. She was going to be right here, every day? How would I survive that without getting to touch her?

"I told you guys I wanted a live-in. With the baby coming, I can't clean your shit up like I used to. She and her sisters are going to take the guesthouse." She narrowed her eyes on us all. "Lucy is only six, so please try to watch your language around her."

Six? So young. I wondered if she looked like Layla. "I'll watch my mouth," I promised. We had made that mistake with Emmie while she was growing up. She could put sailors to shame with her vocabulary. Sure, she had heard it from her mother daily, but we should have at least attempted to get her to not repeat those words.

The others agreed as well. Emmie pushed her half-finished burger away. "Good. I'm counting on you guys. This will be good practice before the baby gets here." She took a sip of her milk. "So, which of you will volunteer to help Layla and her sisters move in on Saturday?"

The other three guys groaned, but I was quick to offer my help. I wasn't about to turn down the chance to spend more time with the little goddess.

Chapter 6
Layla

If I was depressed that I had to go when Jesse had asked me to stay, then I was even more so the rest of the week. I didn't see him at all on Thursday or Friday because the band was spending so much time in the studio. I hated that I went home both evenings with a heavy heart because I hadn't gotten even a little peek at the sexy rocker.

Lana noticed my downbeat attitude and asked me if something was wrong. It was Friday night and we were sitting on our little couch in the living room sharing the rest of the pizza I had picked up for dinner on my way home. Lucy was already in bed, and I was happy to have some us time with Lana. She saw way too much sometimes, and I knew I couldn't keep my feelings about the rocker from her, especially since we were going to be living right next door to the guy.

"What's wrong, Layla?" she asked. "Aren't you liking your new job?"

I shrugged. "The job is great. Emmie is the best boss I have ever had. I just..." I grimaced and shrugged my shoulders again "...I don't know."

Her eyes narrowed. "You act like a girl who is crushing on someone who doesn't know she's alive. Is it one of those rockers?" Lana had a bigger thing about rockers and relationships than I did. That was probably my fault because I had left her to deal with our mother's shit alone when Lydia had kicked me out at sixteen. Poor Lana, who was only nine at the time, had to grow up fast because I wasn't there anymore to take care of her like I had always done from the day she was born.

I had promised the girls when they moved it with me that I wouldn't ever lie to them about anything, so I told Lana about Jesse and how I was feeling. It felt good to talk about it, and she helped me get it a little straighter in my head. I realized I needed to be extra careful. I couldn't start something with Jesse Thornton. Not only was it dangerous because I technically worked for him, but it was dangerous to my emotional well-being as well.

THE ROCKER THAT SAVORS ME

I had to keep my distance. It was a complete surprise to wake up Saturday morning to him knocking on my apartment door. Emmie had promised me that she would have someone help us move, but I thought she meant actual movers or something. Not the band!

But no, that wasn't the case. Jesse Thornton was actually there with Drake Stevenson right behind him looking hung over. "Good morning, beautiful," Jesse greeted me with a grin and an up and down appraisal of my shorts and tank top clad body. His eyes lingered on my legs a little longer, taking in the tattoo that wrapped around and around my right leg.

"Jesse, hey." I was enjoying my own once over of his delicious body. The way his gray tee shirt stretched tightly over his broad chest and how his jeans hung low on his lean hips. His head was shaved smooth, and I ached to run my tongue over it. Fuck! I had to stop or I was going to have to find myself a dry pair of panties.

Drake cleared his throat. "Sometime today, Jess. Stop eye fucking the chick and let's get this show started man."

I couldn't help the blush that crept into my cheeks, but I stepped back and let them enter my small apartment. "I wasn't expecting you guys to help me."

"Neither were we," Drake grumbled as he dropped down on my old, worn couch.

Jesse grinned. "What Drake means is that he is here under duress. This is his punishment for pissing Emmie off last night."

"I still don't understand what I did," he said. "One minute she's all smiles and the next she's screaming at me." He shook his dark head, causing his hair to fall in his face. "I hate pregnancy hormones. Cannot wait for that demon child to get out of her!"

I couldn't help but laugh at him. "That isn't going to help. After the baby is born, she's going to be worse. Take my word for it, sweetie. Postpartum is worse than the mood swings she's having now."

"Ah, hell," both men muttered.

"Hey, Layla, did you already pack the bathroom?" Lana came out of the bedroom with a frown on her face, not yet noticing the men standing in our living room. "I need..." She broke off when she spotted Jesse standing at the end of the couch. "Oh..."

Jesse's brows rose when he saw her. I watched his eyes grow wide when he got his first look at my sister's beauty. Her long midnight black hair was pulled back into a ponytail. Her eyes, an almost amber color, were large. Her nose was ever so slightly upturned at the tip, and her lips looked bee stung and plump. With her long and slender body and those boobs that I knew most girls would have paid thousands to have, she was what I had always wanted to look like. Seriousl,y I didn't know how she had made it through school without a boyfriend, but I was sure it had something to do with her ability to freeze fire with her glare.

"Lana, this is Jesse." I introduced him with a smile. "And that's Drake." I pointed to the couch. "Guys, this is my *seventeen* year old sister, Lana."

I watched Jesse closely while I introduced them, but other than giving her a once over, he seemed to dismiss her beauty. "It's nice to meet you, Lana." He nodded.

"Yeah, you too." There was a slight pink tinting in her cheeks. "Layla, can you help me with something in the bathroom?"

Lucy was parked on the bed, still half asleep. I was glad that we were already packed up for the most part, but there were still a few things that needed to be put in boxes. "Hey, Lucy. Go introduce yourself to Jesse and Drake," I told her, and she climbed off the bed slowly to go do as I asked.

"What's wrong?" I asked as I entered the bathroom behind Lana.

Her cheeks were still pink, but she just needed me to unpack a few girl things for her. By the time I returned to the living room, Lucy was on the sofa between Jesse and Drake, talking animatedly to them. That surprised me because the little girl was normally reserved around men. But there she was asking them all kinds of questions about the new house she was going to be living in.

"That's so awesome!" she said. "Will you build a sandcastle with me, Mr. Drake?"

"Um...Sure." He seemed a little out of his element, but I was touched that he was at least making an effort with her. "We will have to go shopping for some toys though, I think. I'm not sure we have the right tools for sandcastle building."

"Not today, Lucy," I interrupted. "We have a lot to do today, baby."

"Tomorrow?"

Before I could say anything Drake was already nodding his head. "Tomorrow. It's a date, okay?"

Lucy's eyes were huge in her little face. "Promise?"

"Promise." He stood, a smile on his handsome face. "Now, let's get you ladies moved."

Jesse

I didn't realize three females would have so much stuff. Emmie had spoiled me because she always packed light when we traveled. Between Layla, Lana, and Lucy's clothes, and countless other things, the back of the truck that we had rented for the day was pretty full.

I drove the truck back to Malibu with Layla and her sisters following behind. Drake, who had been half dead on the ride out, was now more alive than I had seen him in…Months? Years? I couldn't honestly remember the last time I had seen him really smile like he had been for the last two hours. I couldn't tell if it was because of the way little Lucy seemed to take one look at him and attach herself to him, or… I wasn't going to think those thoughts. Drake would never—I mean never, ever—touch Lana. If there was anyone the teen was safe with, it would be Drake. I couldn't get over how at ease he seemed despite the headache he had been bitching about just hours before. It was good to see him like that because Drake was just so messed up in the head the majority of the time.

When we reached the beach house, he jumped out of the moving truck and got right into helping unload it. Shane and Nik came out to help, and it didn't take as long to unload as it had to fill it up. By the time we had all of their things in the guesthouse, it was after noon and we were all hungry and thirsty.

Emmie had the patio already set up with beers, iced tea, sodas, and several boxes of pizzas for us. I steered clear of the box that had bacon written on top and dived into the one that was loaded down with everything else. Lana and Lucy were already being welcomed by the other guys with good-natured teasing, and I saw that Lucy seemed to be invading more than just Drake's heart as the afternoon went by.

I knew what they saw when they looked at Lucy. I saw the exact same thing. We all saw Emmie who had only been a little younger when she had moved into the trailer park beside of Nik. There was a huge difference between Emmie then and Lucy now. Emmie had been a neglected, abused, lost little girl that was skittish around the four teens that attempted to take her under our wings. Lucy was a healthy, loved little girl.

Lucy was what Emmie should have been.

"There must be a place around here where we can buy all the things we need to make the perfect sandcastle," Drake said to Lucy, who was still munching on pretzels after the three slices of cheese pizza she had already devoured. "Want to go with me to find it?" I felt Layla tense beside me. I didn't know if it was because she felt like Lucy was bothering Drake or if she was worried about Lucy being alone with the rocker. Without thinking about it, I captured her hand and gave it a reassuring squeeze. "That sounds like a really fun idea," I agreed before anyone else could say anything. "Then Layla can get some unpacking done without having to worry about Lucy."

She seemed to relax a little after that. It made my chest tight that she took my opinion on the idea to heart and was confident in it. Lucy shot Layla a look. "Can I go, Layla? Please?"

"Sure. As long as you are on your best behavior, baby."

"Awesome." Lucy pumped a fist in the air, and I came to the conclusion that *awesome* was Lucy's favorite word.

"Awesome." Drake pushed back his chair and stood. Lucy put her little hand in his bigger one. Before they turned to leave, Drake glanced down at Lana who was frowning out at the ocean. "Want to join us, Lana?"

She seemed startled that he asked her. A blush crept into her cheeks, making her face glow. She licked her lips like she was nervous and glanced at Layla. "I...I should stay and help Layla unpack."

"If you want to go, then go." Layla was gathering her trash. "I can handle unpacking." She shooed them away with a smile. "Go. Have fun."

Lana was already up before her sister had finished speaking. She grasped Drake's free hand and started tugging him into the house. The look on my friend's face was priceless, and for the second time I wondered...but no! Drake would never...

When they disappeared inside, I glanced over at Emmie who was still gazing after the three. Her eyes were wide, but there was more wonder in those pretty green eyes than worry. A smile teased her lips, and I let my worry fade away. If Emmie wasn't worried, then I wasn't going to be either.

"Thanks for lunch, guys." Layla had her trash as well as Lana's, Lucy's, and Drake's. She stood up and said, "And thank you for helping us move in. Today has been fun."

"Don't run off," I told her. "Stay. Unpacking can wait a little longer." I didn't want her to go in yet.

"Yes, Layla," Emmie agreed. "Sit and relax. Or go change into a bikini and let's hang out by the pool. I've really enjoyed this afternoon, and I'm not ready for it to be over."

The thought of Layla in a bikini made my dick twitch. I had to bite my cheek to keep from groaning out loud. "I don't know." She looked tempted and I wanted to tempt her more.

I leaned closer and murmured in her ear. "There's a hot tub."

Her chocolate eyes met mine, and I watched as her mouth opened ever so slightly. Her wicked little tongue sneaked out to moisten her bottom lip, and I wanted to suck it into my mouth. "A hot tub?" Her voice came out a little breathless, and I grinned as I nodded.

"Come on, Em," Nik said as he stood and helped Emmie to her feet. "Let's go try on your new bikini. I feel like a dip in the pool myself. Shane, you going to join us?"

"Nah. I'm going into the Hills. Axton is having a party, and I think I'm going to head over and drink up all his scotch." He stood slowly. "See you later, Layla."

"Oh…Bye, Shane."

"Shane, are you staying over?" Emmie called after him.

He shrugged. "Depends. But don't expect me home until tomorrow."

I knew it was coming even before it left her mouth. "Don't drive, Shane. Please don't drive."

He stopped and turned back to her. She pouted at him and Shane was just as much a sucker as the rest of us when it came to that pout. He pulled her close, his hand automatically going to that damned bump and caressing it. "I swear I won't drink and drive, Em." He kissed her cheek.

She hugged him tight then pushed him towards the door. "I'm calling Axton and making sure he gets your keys as soon as you walk through the door."

"Love you, Em," he called as he entered the house.

"Love you, Shane." As soon as he was out of sight, she pulled her phone out and started dialing. Nik looked at me and rolled his eyes before following her into the house while she bitched at Axton about not letting Shane drink and drive.

I watched them go before I turned back to the goddess sitting beside of me. "Do you have a bikini?"

She nodded. "It's a few years old, but yeah, I have one." I could see the anticipation in her eyes. Gods, I loved looking into those eyes! "But it's a little warm for the hot tub. I think I'll stick to the pool."

"I guess we will just have to wait to try it out then." I stood and took the paper plates from her before she could protest. "Go change, Layla. I need to see you in that bikini." I was dying to see her in nothing at all, but right now a bikini would do.

THE ROCKER THAT SAVORS ME

Chapter 7
Layla

By the time I found my bikini and changed into it, twenty minutes had gone by. I grabbed a towel and headed out of the guesthouse. There was a small grassy yard that separated the guesthouse from the main house, and I loved the feel of the thick green grass under my bare feet.

I heard music. It wasn't turned up loud, just enough to provide some background noise. Jesse must have turned it on because he was the only one sitting by the pool. Apparently, Nik and Emmie were still trying on Emmie's new bikini. The realization that I was alone with the sexy rocker in nothing more than a bikini should have made me nervous. Really, it should have, but it didn't.

I tossed my towel on a lounger and dropped down on the edge of the huge pool beside Jesse. He was sticking his bare feet in the water. His eyes were on the ocean on the horizon, but I knew that he had known I was there from the instant I had stepped out onto the deck. His entire body had tensed, just as mine had. There was some unknown force that kept drawing me to this man, and it scared the hell out of me even while it excited me.

"I'm trying not to look," he murmured, keeping his eyes on the horizon. "Because I know the instant I do I won't be able to keep my dick under control."

He might have been trying to keep his eyes off of me, but I had no problem letting mine drink in the sight of his bare chest and back. My fingers actually itched to trace over every hard angle of his sculpted muscles. My mouth was full of saliva from wanting to run my tongue over every fine detail of his many tattoos. And that head! Fuck, I wanted to rub his head to see if it felt as smooth as it looked.

His trunks hung low on his hips and as my gaze traveled over his flat stomach, I saw that he was already having trouble controlling his dick. Without thinking, I raised my hand and was about to touch it when the sliding French doors opened onto the patio, and Nik came out with an ice chest full of beers.

My hand dropped back to my side, my heart racing as I tried to get my desire under control. It was not smart to start something with Jesse Thornton. I was not going to start anything with Jesse Thornton… I really wanted to start something with Jesse Thornton!

"If you make fun of me, I'm going to kick you in the balls," Emmie said as she came out of the house and started up the few steps that lead from the patio to the deck. I thought she looked beautiful with her baby bump sticking out. Her boobs looked full and firm, her ass perfect. From behind no one would even know she was pregnant.

"I think you look beautiful," I assured her as I slipped into the water.

Emmie beamed at me. "Thanks. I wasn't sure if I should wear a bikini, but then I figured I don't give a fuck." She pulled her long auburn hair into a pony tail and turned around. The tattoo on her back caught my attention. I instantly wanted one.

The way the demons wings looked like they were actually a part of her instead of a tattoo. Whoever had done the art work was really freaking talented. Every single scale was precise and well defined, the shadowing done in a way to give it a 3D look. The Gothic style words underneath, "Property of Demon's Wings," was just as beautiful.

"Who did your ink?" I asked, unable to take my eyes off of her back.

"Drake designed it, but I can't remember the guy who put it on." She shrugged. "I got it when I was eighteen in Miami."

"Drake designed it? God, what talent!"

"That's Drake." Emmie stopped beside Jesse who helped her sit down. The way he was so careful with her made something ache inside of me. All of the guys were so careful around Emmie. I didn't think it was just because she was pregnant either. It was as if they treated her like fragile glass. To see those big, bad ass rockers being so gentle around her was something to behold.

"Layla, you want a beer?" Nik asked as he popped the top off of a Corona and offered it to me.

THE ROCKER THAT SAVORS ME

I accepted without hesitation. I didn't drink often, but then again, I found myself doing things lately that I never thought I would ever be doing, like hanging out with rock stars in their swimming pools. For the next hour, we swam and splashed around, and I couldn't ever remember having more fun than I had with those three. It felt as if we had been friends for years. I had only known these people for less than a week. I worked for them, but they were treating me as if I belonged to them. It was another new experience for me.

Emmie sat on the edge of the pool again. Water streamed out of her ponytail and dripped down her body. She was still laughing at Nik's attempt to dunk Jesse, which was no easy thing to do even considering Nik's muscles and height. "Ha, ha," she taunted. "I knew you couldn't do it."

Nik swam over to her and pushed her thighs wide so he could step between them. "You're supposed to be on my side."

She grinned down at him where his head was eye level with her breasts. "Says who?"

"Says me, the one that loves you most." His arms wrapped around her distended waist. "The one that put this little angel in there." He dropped a kiss on her belly, and I saw Emmie shiver. "You remember me, right? The one who's going to marry you when you get around to deciding you actually want to get married."

"I said I would, didn't I?" She ran her fingers through his hair, and the moment seemed too intimate for me to watch so I turned around.

Jesse was standing just behind me. I hadn't heard him swim closer. Even with the cool water washing over me, I couldn't help but melt. His closeness did things to my body that none of the three lovers from my past had been able to do with a touch. The way he looked at me caused air to get trapped in my lungs, and I had to keep reminding myself to breathe.

"I want to kiss you so fucking bad," he muttered under his breath so only I could hear him. Not that he needed to bother. Emmie and Nik were locked at the mouth now, and I doubted they even realized that we were still there.

THE ROCKER THAT SAVORS ME

My lips instantly tingled as if anticipating his kiss.

"But I'll be damned if I'm going to do it here." He ran a hand over his smooth head. Reaching out, his hand captured mine and linked our fingers together. My skin felt like it was sizzling from that innocent contact with his skin.

I wanted him to kiss me! I was ready for him to devour me with that wicked looking mouth of his. My fingers curved around his, and I was taking a step closer when I heard Lana's laugh as she came out of the house. She was followed by Drake, who was laughing just as hard as she was, with Lucy bringing up the rear.

I jumped back as if I were standing to close to a live wire, which I was sure I was. To me, Jesse was like an electrical current that was ready to zap me at any moment. One that would fry me if I stepped to close, something I was about to do.

"I thought you were unpacking," Lana called as she pulled a sucker from her mouth. The three of them all had candy in their mouths and grins on their faces. I hadn't seen Lana smile like that since we were little.

"The pool was just too tempting," I told her as I started climbing out.

"Look, Layla." Lucy came rushing over to me with a bag full of toys. I saw an inflatable raft, swim rings, and several other pool toys. Drake had a bigger bag which I could only assume was filled with the sandcastle tools that they had gone after in the first place. "Drake said that since I don't know how to swim yet, I have to wear these if I want to get in the pool. But he promised he would teach me!"

My heart clenched at how thoughtful Drake was. I shot him a thankful smile. "Thank you, Drake. That was sweet of you."

He shrugged like it was no big deal. "Come on, Lucy. We have a few hours left of daylight. Let's start on that castle."

Leaving the bag with me, she skipped away with him. Her little hand was swallowed in his huge paw as they walked towards the beach, hand in hand. Lana watched after them with a look of pure longing on her face. I didn't know if it was because she wanted to play with them too…or something else. I would have to talk to her about it later.

THE ROCKER THAT SAVORS ME

When the two got to the beach, Drake glanced back, a frown on that face that was almost beautiful. "Lana, are you coming?"

The look of longing was quickly masked behind a grin. "Maybe in a little while. I want to change first."

I couldn't be sure but it looked like disappointment crossed the rocker's face. His smile wasn't as big as it had been when they had gotten back. "Okay."

Yes, I really needed to talk to Lana later!

--

Jesse

It took for fucking ever for my dick to calm down after nearly kissing Layla in the pool. A cold shower hadn't helped. Masturbating hadn't even taken the edge off. I wanted that little goddess to the point of pain, and I wasn't used to denying myself when it came to things I wanted. Damn, I had become spoiled over the last ten years!

Sunday I tried to stay away from her. I told myself I was letting her get settled in, that I didn't want to crowd her. In actuality I was scared shitless. I was sure that I cared about her, and that was terrifying. How could I have feelings for a woman that I just met? How was it that she was constantly on my mind while I was awake? Why was she haunting my dreams while I slept?

By Monday I knew that I needed to do something about how I was feeling. Maybe I should try to get her out of my system. That had to be what was going on. She was something I wanted, and I had been denying myself for days now. If I fucked her out of my system, then this ache in my chest would go away, right?

Fuck, I hoped that was all it was. Relationships scared the hell out of me. None of the ones I had ever seen in the past had worked out. My mom and dad's relationship sure hadn't worked out. I'd never even had one that lasted past a few days, and that had only been about fucking. Terrifyingly enough, I wanted more than that with Layla. I had enjoyed talking to her and getting to know her. I wanted to know what made her laugh—because God that laugh did things to my dick! I wanted to know what made her cry because I never wanted to see tears in her big chocolate eyes.

"Jesse!"

I frowned when I heard Emmie calling for me. I had dropped down on the long part of the sectional when we had gotten home from the studio and must have fallen asleep. The last two nights I hadn't gotten much sleep. Layla had invaded my mind. Fuck, my hand was developing calluses from all the jacking I had done over the last few days. When I did sleep, it was only to wake up with another raging hard on that had to be taken care of or I'd suffer the bluest balls known to man.

"Jesse!" Emmie called out again, and I rubbed a hand over my face to try to clear it of the sleep that still lingered. "Are you in the house?" I heard her soft padding of footsteps and sat up.

"In here, Em," I called back just as she appeared in the doorway of the living room.

She frowned down at me, concern in her green eyes. "Are you okay?"

"Just tired. Haven't been sleeping lately." Her eyes darkened with worry. "I'm fine, Em. I swear. I'm not sick or anything." Just constantly hard because my little goddess was driving me crazy with want!

She still looked worried. "Dinner is ready. Are you hungry?" My stomach grumbled loud enough for her to hear, and her worried expression eased into a small smile. "I'll take that as a yes. Come on, I made meatloaf."

"Not with bacon." I didn't think I could handle bacon tonight.

She laughed. "No. I only put it on a small portion."

I followed her into the dining room where Drake and Shane were already loading their plates down with mashed potatoes, homemade baked mac and cheese, and fresh green beans. Nik was putting a basket of yeast rolls on the table and taking his usual seat. We had been eating homemade meals like this all summer, and I had gotten used to it. I loved sitting down with all the people that mattered to me and sharing food that had been made with some TLC.

Emmie took her place, and I finally sat down between her and Drake. The first bite of one of the rolls made me groan. "God, Em. This is amazing."

THE ROCKER THAT SAVORS ME

"Thanks, but I didn't make them." She was drizzling a little ketchup over her bacon crusted meatloaf. "Layla helped me out in the kitchen before heading out. I'll let her know that you like them."

Layla. Just the sound of her name made my dick twitch, and I took my time savoring the rest of my roll and two more. Conversations were going on around me, and I tried to keep up with them, but I was too consumed with thoughts of Layla to pay close attention to what was being said.

"Jesse, can you do it?"

My head snapped up at Nik's question. He was frowning at me as if he were worried about me. I sighed and realized I had missed an entire conversation that probably had been important. "Sorry, man. What?"

"Em has a doctor's appointment in the morning. Can you take her since we don't really need you in the studio tomorrow?"

"You know I will." I pushed my plate away and reached for my barely touched beer. "What time do we need to leave, sweetheart?"

She shrugged. "About ten thirty. So you can sleep in if you want."

"Sounds good." I didn't mind going with Emmie to the doctor. I meant that I got to hear the baby's heartbeat, and it never failed to move me. My little 'niece' had already invaded my heart.

As soon as he was finished with dinner, Drake stood and muttered an excuse. I figured he was going to go hit a new bottle of Jack Daniels. When he was out the door, we all shared a dark look but went back to our food. I hated that my friend was so dependent on a bottle to get through the night. I hated even more his reasons for needing it.

Pushing those dark thoughts away, I helped Nik clear the table. We filled the dishwasher but didn't turn it on because neither of us really knew what was what on the stupid thing. I shut the door and turned to find Nik pulling a beer out of the fridge. "Want one?" he asked.

"Nah, man. I'm good." I wasn't in the mood for more beer. Instead, I pulled a can of coke from the fridge and popped the top.

THE ROCKER THAT SAVORS ME

The sugary soda woke me up, at least for the moment, and I followed Nik out onto the patio where Emmie was already curled up on one of the loungers looking up at the star filled sky.

It was cooler out and Nik spread a thin throw over the both of them as he sat beside her and pulled her close. I leaned back in my chair and closed my eyes, enjoying the sound of surf crashing on the beach. Shane came out mumbling something about a run but no one bothered to say anything as he headed down the beach.

It was so peaceful that I started to drift off. Then the sound of laughter from the yard caught my attention and my eyes snapped open. It was a rare sound, one that I hadn't heard to its full extent in what felt like forever, but I knew who it was.

Drake was laughing—a sound so happy that it had to come from his very soul.

When the laugh was followed by a very feminine giggle, my hackles rose and I glanced over at Emmie who had sat up straight in the lounger. Our eyes met. Mine were filled with a mixture of emotions. I knew who was giggling, and it wasn't Layla whose laugh went straight to my dick. I knew that Lana was safe with Drake. We all did. But was Drake safe with Lana?

Emmie's face was full of wonder, and I saw tears glaze her eyes. Her hand covered her mouth. "Oh my Gods!" she whispered. "He's laughing!"

I stood, needing to see what the two were up to. I had to know what they were doing that was making Drake so happy. At the edge of the patio, I peeked my head around to look into the small yard that separated the house from the guesthouse. There were two dozen little candles spread over the sheet that they had spread on the ground. In the dim lighting, Drake was sketching something in one of his many sketchbooks while Lana sat across from him just smiling at him.

I stepped back before they could see me, my heart in my throat. Oh fuck! I didn't know what to feel right then, but this overwhelming sense of wonder was coursing through me. Drake never—and I mean NEVER—shared his artistic skills with anyone. He only ever used them to paint and draw out his nightmares. The fact he was drawing Lana, that obscenely beautiful girl with the bell-like giggles, was nothing short of a miracle.

I dropped down onto the chair I had been in earlier and rubbed my hands over my head. What did I do? How could I step in when he seemed so happy and was doing things that were so un-Drake like? How could I break that up when I had never seen my friend so... My head snapped around as a realization hit me.

"He isn't drinking!" I whispered and glanced over at Emmie and Nik. "He's back there drawing with her and he doesn't have a bottle with him."

They both sat up at that news. The two shared a long look then slowly grinned as a grin spread across my own face. Maybe Lana was just the thing that Drake needed. I wasn't going to step in. Not right now. Until Drake gave me a reason to doubt him, I wasn't going anywhere near those two.

Chapter 8
Layla

I spent all day Sunday unpacking and getting the guesthouse cleaned up. There was plenty to do, and I was thankful for the distraction from my crazy thoughts of Jesse. Of course I wasn't disappointed that he didn't come over to talk. I was relieved even.

Okay, so I was heart sick that he didn't seek me out. I craved being near him, even for just a minute. I was so messed up that I didn't know what to do about it. My desire for him was far and beyond anything that I had ever experienced before in my life.

Sunday night, while Lana finished up the rest of her homework, I took a moment to talk to her about Drake. She just laughed it off and said that they were friends. She promised me she wasn't going to get involved with a rocker, but there was something like longing in her amber eyes, and I felt my stomach clench with worry.

I didn't push the subject, though. I would just watch Lana and Drake and make sure that my little sister wasn't getting in deeper than she could handle. I didn't want Lana falling for a rocker. *I didn't want to fall for a rocker…*

Monday, I had to take an hour off so I could get Lucy situated at the local school. When I got back I rushed through my routine for the upstairs. I vacuumed the halls and stairs then quickly took care of Drake's room.

The covers were thrown all over the place, but they didn't smell like they normally did. There was still the distinct scent of fear on the sheets but not like I had grown used to the week before. When I got to the bathroom, I marveled at how clean it still was. There was the faint odor of vomit, but not the overwhelming stench I had cleaned up morning after morning the week before.

Before I left for the day, I helped Emmie out in the kitchen, teaching her how to make the yeast rolls I had learned to make from my first boyfriend's mother. When I looked at the clock and saw that it was nearly time for the guys to get home from the studio, I retreated to the guesthouse. I had gone two days without seeing Jesse now. It had been difficult, but I had somehow managed not to think about him every five minutes. I didn't want to mess up the progress I was making.

Lucy needed help with her math, so I sat down at the kitchen table after dinner to help her. She was amazing at reading and was already on a fifth grade reading level, but math just blew her mind. Not that I could say anything. Math wasn't my strongest subject either. I despaired at what was going to happen when she got into high school. I would have to hire a tutor or something for her because I sure as hell wouldn't be much help to her.

By ten, Lucy was in bed and Lana came inside. I hadn't said anything when she had gathered up all our candles and an old sheet and disappeared outside. The sound of her giggles and Drake's deep laughter had actually been heartwarming, but I still worried. When Lana gave me the brightest smile I had ever seen coming from her, I just wished her a good night and settled in on the hide-a-bed in the living room while she went into the bedroom that she shared with Lucy.

I drifted off to sleep, proud of myself for not thinking of Jesse all day long…only to dream about him!

Lana's alarm woke me from a particularly wet dream, and I sat up, my breathing ragged as I pressed shaking fingers to my throbbing clit. Lana was in the shower, so I had a few minutes to take care of the ache that dreaming of Jesse had caused. I closed my eyes, picturing his smooth head between my legs as his tongue licked my pussy until I couldn't hold on any longer.

Using my thumb to press down on the top of my clit while I thrust two fingers into my soaking wet pussy, I bit my lip to keep from whimpering in pure pleasure as I felt my inner muscles start to clench and convulse. When I could breathe again, I sucked my fingers into my mouth, imagining it was Jesse's dick, as I licked off my juices from his thick cock. When my fingers were clean of my arousal, I got up to start my day.

Lana was just getting out of the shower when I entered the bathroom. Her hair was dripping all over the place, and she wrapped a towel around it before reaching for another to wrap around her gorgeous body. She wasn't tattooed or pierced like I was. She had virgin skin, and I wanted to keep it that way, but she had already hinting at getting one for her birthday in a few weeks.

"Can I have some gas money, Layla?" Lana asked as she rushed to get dry. "Your car is low."

I washed my hands. "Of course. But I don't have any cash. Just use my credit card at the pump, okay?" I reached for a ponytail holder and pulled my thick hair back into a messy bun before reaching for my tooth brush.

"Thanks, Layla." She ran a wide toothed comb through her damp hair then went into the bedroom to get dressed. "Hey, do you care if I have dinner with Drake Friday?"

My hand froze with the toothbrush still in my mouth. My mouth was full of toothpaste and spit, but I moved to the door and frowned at my sister as she pulled on jeans and a simple black tank top over her black bra. "What?" Maybe I hadn't heard her right.

Lana pulled her damp hair out of the shirt and turned to face me. "I want to have dinner with Drake Friday night. He asked me to go to this little Greek place that he thinks I will like. I promise I won't be out late."

"Lana, he's in his thirties," I reminded her around my mouth full of toothpaste. "And he's a rocker."

She sighed. "He isn't like those guys that Mom played around with, Layla. Yes, I'm sure he's lived hard, but there is something about him that…" she shook her head "…I don't know what it is, Layla. I feel like there is this invisible rope that pulls me towards him."

"Lana…"

"No. Please, just listen. I like him. But right now we're just friends. He isn't ready for anything more…" I opened my mouth to ask how she knew that when she went on. "We haven't talked about it, if that's what you want to know. I just sense it. He's haunted by something in his past and until he's ready to face it, he won't be ready for me. So, please just trust me. Okay? I want to be his friend."

I shut my mouth, my teeth biting into my bottom lip while I tried not to swallow the mess in my mouth. I trusted Lana. She was a good girl with a good head on her shoulders, and in a few short weeks she was going to be eighteen, an adult. I had to trust that she knew what she was doing and would be able to handle any mistakes she might happen to make along the way.

"Okay, Lana. I trust you to know what is best for yourself. Just be careful, okay? And remember that he's still a rocker. That isn't going to change."

--

After I had put Lucy on the bus, I headed into the house. The guys were already gone; I had heard them leave right after Lana pulled away. I relaxed in the knowledge that other than Emmie, who was either still asleep or in her office working, I was alone in the house.

The first thing I did was take care of Drake's room. His sheets weren't as rumpled this morning, but there was still the slight smell of fear and sweat, so I changed his sheets and tossed his comforter in the washer before taking care of his bathroom.

When I was done upstairs, I straightened up the kitchen. The dishwasher was full of dirty dishes, and I turned it on before getting out a pan to fry up some bacon for Emmie. I knew she would be hungry, but if she was working, she would forget about eating unless I brought her something.

I fried up the bacon nice and crispy, just the way she liked, and scrambled some eggs while the bread toasted. I was just plating up the eggs when I heard footsteps entering the kitchen behind me. "Hey, little momma. Are you hungry?" I asked without turning around.

"Starving."

I nearly dropped the skillet at the sound of Jesse's deep voice. I yelped and turned my head to find him standing in front of the island in nothing more than a pair of jeans that sat almost indecently low on those narrow hips. My mouth went dry as my pussy flooded with desire.

Good God! He was something from a dark fantasy. Sure, I had seen his chest when we were swimming on Saturday, but that didn't mean I was any less affected right now. That broad, thickly muscled chest with the black heart over his left pectoral. The hard abs that were all hard angles and deep ridges. The little trail of dark

THE ROCKER THAT SAVORS ME

hair that narrowed from his belly button down his flat stomach and disappeared into his jeans…

I closed my gaping mouth and tried to steady my racing heart as I turned away from the devastating sight of the sexy man behind me. "Um…I wasn't expecting you to be here." I got out in a voice that only slightly shook with my need.

"Em has a doctor's appointment and I was the only one free to go." I heard his footsteps as he came around the island. My already crazy heart rate accelerated as I sensed him stop just behind me. I could actually feel the heat radiating from his big body. "Can I join you for breakfast?"

"Of course. Just let me make some more eggs." I reached for the carton of eggs with a hand that trembled.

His hand caught my elbow, and he carefully pulled me around to face him. All the oxygen seemed to leave the room as I looked up into those eyes that changed with every emotion that crossed his endearing face. Right now, they were darker than I had ever seen them. "I was hoping for something a little sweeter than eggs, Layla," he murmured as his head lowered towards mine.

It was stupid. It was crazy…but I had never been all that smart or sane. At least that was what I told myself as I stepped closer. He towered over me, but I thought we fit perfectly against each other. His erection pressed against my stomach, my breasts against his chest in just the right spot. I could see the pulse beating at the base of his throat, and I ached to suck on it.

"You are so fucking beautiful," he growled, his head making a slow dive towards mine as if he were giving me time to reconsider letting him kiss me.

The first brush of his lips across mine was soft and gentle, but no less intoxicating. His lower lip was fuller than his top, and before I could think about it, I latched on to it, sucking it into my mouth to get the full taste of him. It was like a drug, that sweet addicting taste of passionate man. Large fingers gripped my pony tail, holding my head still while he explored my mouth with his tongue.

A moan escaped us both when he pulled back. I pressed closer, wanting his mouth. He turned his head away, cursing softly while he tried to suck in deep breath after deep breath. The kiss hadn't been long, maybe twenty seconds or so, but it had stolen his breath completely. I was thrilled knowing that I had affected him so completely.

One big hand rubbed over my jean clad hips and pulled me into his hard body. His erection throbbed against my stomach, making me burn for him. I laid my head on his chest, loving the sound of his out of control heartbeat. It matched my own and let me know that I wasn't the only one fighting for control over this thing that was between us.

After a few minutes of him holding me like that, he stepped back enough so there was a few inches of space between us. His hand was still on my hip, though, and I looked up at him through my lashes. "I knew you were going to blow my mind, Layla," he murmured in a passion filled voice, "but I had no idea that you would bring me close to blowing my load with just a kiss." He brushed a soft kiss across my forehead. "I've never been that affected by a kiss. Not even when I was fifteen and experimenting for the first time."

"I'm pretty affected myself," I assured him in a quiet voice.

Those eyes darkened even more, and I longed to chart them, to watch while he experienced every emotion known to man and witness how many colors they could actually turn. "Have dinner with me tonight," he whispered, lowering his head to brush a tender kiss across my cheek. "I promise not to seduce you unless you ask me too."

That could be a problem because I was sure that I wanted him to seduce me. I licked my lips. "I...I can't tonight," I whispered, regret clouding my voice. "Lucy has school in the morning and I...I want to, but..."

"Shhh..." He kissed my other cheek, just the barest touch of warm damp lips to my soft skin. "Okay, not tonight. Saturday then. Dinner. Maybe a few drinks at this bar that has live bands?" I nodded slowly. "I can do Saturday."

Another kiss, this one to the tip of my nose. "I can't wait." Then he stepped back, his hand moving to his crotch to adjust himself. I watched unashamed as he tucked it into a more comfortable position. Fuck me!

Just as he stepped back, Emmie's voice came from the direction of the office. She was on the phone but walking towards the kitchen. "If that's what it takes, that's what you have to do. No, that's not acceptable. Make sure it gets done!"

She was muttering to herself as she entered the kitchen. Either she didn't feel the sexual tension in the room or was ignoring it as she went to the stove and lifted a strip of crispy bacon from the paper towel lined plate that I had placed it on to drain. "Do you know how hard it is to get stupid people to do smart things?" she asked no one in particular.

"How hard is it, Em?" Jesse asked casually as he moved around the island and sat down.

"Near fucking impossible." She rubbed her hand over her distended stomach while she shoved another strip of bacon into her mouth. "But that's just my luck today."

I cleared my throat of the remaining desire and turned back to the eggs. "Can I fix you something, Jesse?"

"That would be great, Layla." He was watching me, and I had to fight my desire to turn around and look at him while I scrambled his eggs. When I started to place some bacon on his plate he stopped me. "No, please no. I can't stomach bacon."

Emmie laughed. "Poor baby."

"It's all your fault, too!" he accused as I placed his plate in front of him. "I hate the very smell of bacon now. How can you stand to eat it on everything, Em?"

She shrugged, shoving yet another strip into her mouth. "The baby wants it, so the baby is going to get it."

Jesse

I woke the way I had the last several mornings with an erection that was on the verge of painful and my hand working it as the remnants of my dream flashed behind my closed lids.

Layla on her knees as she sucked my cock. Her hair wrapped around my hands as I thrust into her hot, fuckable mouth. She swallowed half of me, and I could feel the back of her throat as I

THE ROCKER THAT SAVORS ME

slid down—damn the girl had no gag reflex! I squeezed my dick harder and pulled down on the sac beneath, trying to make the pleasure last as I jacked at a speed that should have made my dick catch on fire.

With a muffled shout, I erupted into my hand, my breathing ragged, my heart racing. I had to have that little goddess. I had to have her soon!

A shave and a shower, and then I pulled on my jeans before going in search of some breakfast. The fact that I had heard Layla moving around in Drake's room a little while ago made me take my time shaving. The thought of seeing her made me hard again despite the release I had brought myself just a short while ago.

When I found her making breakfast I couldn't resist having a taste of her sweet lips. I needed to know if they tasted as good as they seemed to in my dreams. Fuck, I hadn't expected her kiss to make me practically blow my wad then and there. A simple kiss, innocent enough, but it had packed the force of a hurricane I was so blown away from it.

I was disappointed when she turned me down for dinner, but I understood her reasons. I could also see that she really wanted to go out with me. It scared the fuck out of me because I had never been on a date before. Being a rocker didn't require me to wine and dine a chick before I fucked her brains out. I still asked her out. Layla deserved the wine and dine treatment, even if all we were doing was grabbing dinner and seeing a local band at a bar.

"I hate this," Emmie muttered as she scooted back on the exam table. She was naked from the waist down with a sheet over her legs. When the nurse had asked her how she was feeling, Emmie had admitted to feeling some pressure low in her hips. The next thing I knew she was telling Em to strip.

I had turned my back to give her some privacy. It felt wrong to see Emmie naked now when it hadn't in the past. Hell, I had seen that girl naked more than any other female that had ever been in my life, but there had never been even a twinge from my dick at the sight of her nakedness. Sure, I had appreciated the view; the girl was smoking hot. When it came to my other head, he was completely lifeless when presented with her naked body. Now that she was pregnant, with my best friend's kid no less, I felt a little perverted seeing her female parts.

"What are they going to do?" I asked, unsure what to expect.

Emmie made a sour face. "Oh, nothing really. They are just going to put their fingers in there and see if I'm dilated or something."

I blanched at the thought of watching someone putting their hands on and in my Emmie. Suddenly, I wished that I had gone into the studio and insisted that Nik take her to this thing. There was a knock on the door and a man in his late forties walked in with a frown on his face and his glasses half way down his long nose.

"Good afternoon, Miss Jameson." The doctor greeted us in a professional tone as he looked down at her files.

"Doctor Chesterfield."

The doctor raised his head and gave me a once over before offering me his hand. "You must be one of Emmie's *guys*." He gave me a half smile.

I shook his hand. "Jesse."

"Good to meet you." He dropped down onto his chair with the chart in his hand, his attention fully focused on Emmie now. "So, you have been having some pressure. How long has it been going on?"

Emmie shrugged. "A day or so. Nothing too horrible. Just really uncomfortable," she explained.

Dr. Chesterfield nodded. "Well your urine was clear. No infection. Let's take a look to see how the baby is positioned." He pulled on some gloves and then positioned Emmie so she was lying on her back with her feet in some scary contraption called stirrups. He raised the paper blanket to her knees, and she spread her legs wide.

Emmie reached for my hand, and I was quick to let her grab on. She clenched it tight while the doctor moved around down there. A small whimper escaped her mouth, and I was about to punch the doctor when he pulled back and tossed the gloves in the trash. He was frowning, and I felt dread fill my stomach.

THE ROCKER THAT SAVORS ME

"Well?" Emmie muttered as she sat up, holding the paper blanket to her waist.

The doctor was washing his hands now, but he turned around to face her while he dried them. "The baby's head is already large. That's going to be a big baby, Emmie. And you aren't exactly made to deliver a child like that."

"What does that mean?" she whispered.

He gave her a reassuring smile. "It just means that I think you should have a C-section. It will be best for both you and the baby. You are a small little thing, and after seeing the baby's father on your last appointment, I can assume that she is going to take after him."

Tears came on so suddenly I didn't have time to prepare for their impact as she rubbed her hands over her belly. "I had just gotten used to the thought of pushing her out. Now you're saying I have to be cut open?" She scrubbed a hand over her face. "I hate this," she whispered, and I pulled her against my chest.

"I know it's scary to think about, Emmie. Let me explain what will happen so you will be a little more prepared, okay?" The doctor told us exactly how he would perform the C-section, or cesarean section, or whatever it was! I felt the blood drain from my face as he described how he would cut Emmie open and move her insides around before pulling the baby out. Emmie would be awake during the whole thing.

Fuck, I really wished Nik had come!

Emmie was quiet the entire drive home. When her phone rang, she just turned the ringer off and tossed it in her purse. I drove with one hand on the wheel and the other holding one of her hers. She clutched at it as if it was her only life line, and I couldn't blame her because I was holding on just as tightly.

My phone rang just as I was pulling into the driveway at home. I glanced down to see Nik's face on the screen and snatched it up as soon as the car was in park. "Come home," I told him without bothering to offer a greeting. "Emmie's okay, but just get home."

THE ROCKER THAT SAVORS ME

There was a charged pause, and then Nik muttered a string of violent curses. "I'm on my way. She's okay, right? You swear to me she's okay, Jesse!"

I ran a hand over my face and head. "She's fine, Nik. She's just upset."

Another charged pause before he asked in an emotion filled question. "The baby..?"

"She's fine too. Just hurry the fuck up, Nik," I told him and ended the call. I turned in my seat to find Emmie just staring out the window at the beach house. I reached for her chin and gently turned her to face me. "This isn't that bad," I murmured. "Women have C-sections all the time, sweetheart."

She gave me a small smile. "I guess they do." She sighed. "This is just really hard to take in, you know?"

"I know." I couldn't think about what would happen when it came time for the baby to be born. The doctor was already talking about a possible date to take the baby. Depending on how the baby was doing, he wanted to take her at least a week before November 6th, Emmie's due date.

Which meant that the baby was coming earlier than expected!

I got out and helped Emmie from the car. She held onto my hand as we entered the house. She sat on the long end of the sectional, and I offered to get her some iced water. She just shrugged and I rushed to do it—to do anything to feel helpful right now!

Layla was in the kitchen when I walked in. She was putting away dishes and offered me a shy smile as I entered the room. The smile evaporated when she saw my pale, drawn face.

"What's wrong?" she demanded.

I sighed, wanting to tell her everything. She looked thoughtful as I moved around fixing Emmie a glass of iced water while I told her how the doctor's appointment had gone. When I was done, she just smiled and left the kitchen. I found her sitting by Emmie in the living room.

Emmie was sobbing while Layla held her close, gently rocking her. "I know it's scary, Emmie. I would be terrified too, honey."

THE ROCKER THAT SAVORS ME

I had never seen Emmie cling like that to another female before. It was gut wrenching to watch her crying, but I was glad that it was Layla holding her close, whispering soothing words to her while she got it all out of her system. Emmie had never had a friend that could help her through female things like this. Even though the guys and I would move mountains for her, we had never been able to soothe her like Layla was now.

"I bet it's on YouTube," Layla said once Emmie had calmed enough that she was no longer sobbing. Dammit, those little hiccup noises were just as bad if you asked me. "And if not, we could get you a tape of an actual C-section. I bet the doctor made it sound terrifying. I think seeing it will help you understand better. Lana was born by C-section and my mom said it was much better than having me the old fashioned way."

"I'm so scared, Layla," she whispered.

I wanted to punch something. Emmie had had enough fear growing up. I promised her and myself that she would never have to be scared again the day she came to live with us. There was nothing I could do about the fear she was feeling right now. There was no one that I could destroy to make her fear go away this time. I was useless right now, and it was killing me.

"Every woman is scared when she's having a baby, Em. I swear that what you're feeling is natural. It's going to be okay. You and the baby are going to be just fine." Layla was stroking her hair, moving it from her damp face, offering gentle smiles and tender words.

"Let's get your computer and check out some sites," Layla said. She glanced up at me, gave me a reassuring smile, and held out her hand for the glass of water I clutched tightly in my hand. It was a wonder I hadn't broken the glass the way I was holding it. Her fingers lingered just a moment longer than necessary on my hand, but in that moment I felt some of my tension ease. "How about getting Emmie's laptop for us?" she murmured.

Finally something I could do! I nodded and practically sprinted down the hall to get Emmie's computer. When I returned she was sipping the water and her tears had mostly dried up. Layla took the computer from me with a smile and opened it. I stood there, not sure what to do, while the girls pulled up site after site on C-sections.

When I heard a baby crying, I stepped behind the sectional and crouched down so I could watch too. There was a woman lying on a table, a tent separating her head from the rest of her body. Several people wearing surgical scrubs stood on either side of the woman's stomach while the one I assumed was the doctor worked on the woman. "Going to feel some pressure," The doctor told the woman.

The whole thing only took minutes. When it was over, there was another screaming baby. Apparently, the woman had been carrying twins. A nurse took the baby from the doctor, wrapped it up in a blanket, and showed it to the mother.

"What do you think?" Layla dared to ask after the video had stopped.

Emmie shook her head. "It's still scary…but you were right. The doctor made it sound much scarier than the video showed it to be."

"Well, Nik will be there with you," Layla assured her. "You get to have someone back in the operating room with you. Nik will make sure that you are fine. Right, Jesse?"

"Fuck yes, he will." I gripped Emmie's shoulder, giving it a little squeeze. "You and the baby are going to be just fine, sweetheart. I promise."

The front door opened and slammed shut. I figured Nik had to have broken every traffic law in the state to get home so quickly. It was just a little over an hour's drive to the studio with traffic. Nik had managed it in half that. "Baby?" he called out, sounding frantic.

"I'm here," Emmie called.

He fell on his knees in front of her, his hair looking crazy, his face pale, and his eyes blood shot. "Fuck, Em. Tell me what's going on?" His voice was thick with emotion. "I've been going out of my mind…"

Layla stood and I followed her from the room while Emmie told Nik about the visit to the doctor. She glanced at me over her shoulder as she walked towards the kitchen. "You look like you could use a drink," she murmured softly.

"Or ten." I ran a hand over my face and head.

She grinned. "Come on. I'll fix you something."

Before she could enter the kitchen, I grabbed her waist and pushed her up against the wall without turning her around. I held onto her tight, needing her against me but too much of a coward to turn her around so she wouldn't see the tears in my eyes. "Thank you, Layla," I whispered against her ear and felt her shiver. "Thank you for helping Emmie."

THE ROCKER THAT SAVORS ME

Chapter 9
Layla

If I thought the kiss from that morning was hot, it was nothing compared to having Jesse pressing me against the wall felt with his chest against my back, his dick snug against my ass. My breasts pressed against the wall while my nipple rings tugged with every breath I took in.

His fingers skimmed down my bare arms causing goose flesh to pop up with every stroke of those big thick fingers. "Thank you, Layla." He breathed against my ear, and I couldn't help but shiver. "Thank you for helping Emmie."

The sincerity in his voice and the gratitude spoke more to me than anything else. I had seen the way he was with Emmie, the way they all were. It hadn't really hit me how much that girl was loved until right now. It made my heart ache with an emotion I had never felt before in my life. This big rocker, a man that I had seen rocking hard on television and in the tabloids, could feel so deeply for another human being was amazing to me.

My experiences with rockers had never shown me that that type of person could feel such emotions.

Hot, slightly damp lips grazed my exposed neck. "Really, Layla. Thank you." He stepped back and quietly walked away.

I stood there for a long while trying to get my body to stop trembling. Good God, that man made me ache without even trying! My whole body was one massive throb, and my heart was trying to break through my chest it was beating so hard.

On shaking legs, I made it to the downstairs bathroom and splashed cool water on my face and ran my wrists under the stream of slightly chilled water. I didn't look at myself in the mirror, too frightened of what I might find in my eyes, too much of a coward to let myself admit that I had feelings for the rocker that went beyond lust.

--

The rest of the week passed quickly enough. I worked hard, made sure that the house was spotless, and then made sure I was out of the main house before the guys returned from the studio each evening.

Lana disappeared every night after dinner, sometimes taking her homework with her, and didn't return until it was bed time. Sometimes I heard their laughter just outside. Other times I would look out the window and see the two walking side by side on the beach. I didn't ask questions, although I knew the smart thing to do was demand to know what she was doing, but like I had told her, I trusted my sister to make the right decisions with Drake.

Friday arrived all too soon for me. I watched Lana as she went through her entire wardrobe and finally settled on something to wear. A simple black skirt with a white camisole and a short sleeved black sweater that only had two buttons to keep it closed. She looked beautiful as always, but when she got into my makeup, I found a much older version of my baby sister looking back at me. I hated it but I kept my mouth shut as I watched Drake whisk her away for their dinner at some Greek restaurant that Lana was supposed to love.

I tried not to watch the clock the whole evening. I hadn't given Lana a curfew, but I hoped she would be responsible enough to know when it was time to call it a night. Lucy attempted to keep me distracted. We played a few of her board games, and I let her cheat the majority of the time. We colored until she was sleepy, and then I tucked her into bed with just one story instead of her normal three.

I was just turning away when her eyes suddenly opened and she clutched my hand. "Do you think Lana likes Drake?"

Her question surprised me. "I don't know, Lucy. Why do you ask?"

She sighed. "Because I like him. I want her to like him too. Drake is really awesome."

I bit my lip to keep from smiling. Lucy didn't give such high praise to just anyone, and *awesome* was as good as it got in her book. "He is kind of cool," I agreed, "and I think that Lana and Drake are going to be great friends."

"Do you think that he will marry her?" She sounded excited about the prospect.

THE ROCKER THAT SAVORS ME

My stomach clenched in fear. "I don't think that is going to happen, honey. Lana needs to go to college. She needs to find herself before she can handle something like that..." I broke off, not wanting to discuss something so heavy with my six year old sister. "Go to sleep now, Lucy. You can ask Lana all about her night in the morning." I placed a kiss on her forehead and made my escape.

It surprised me when Lana opened the front door at just after eleven. I had thought she would be out until at least after midnight. When she shut the door and leaned back against it, I knew that her mind was still on the evening and the man she had spent it with. She had this star struck look on her face and wonder lit her eyes.

I cleared my throat to grab her attention, and she glanced over at me sitting on the sofa. A grin split her beautiful face, and it was so infectious I couldn't help smiling back. "So it went well?"

She practically floated over to the sofa and dropped down beside me. She kicked off the heels she had borrowed and laid her feet across my lap while she leaned back with a content sigh. "I had a blast. He has this way of making everyone else but me seem insignificant. There were three girls at the restaurant trying to get him to notice them, but he kept his eyes solely on me. We talked about everything and nothing, just like we always do. Then he took me to this little park, and we just sat on the swings for forever. I didn't want to come home, Lana, but he said he didn't want to get me in trouble..."

The news that it was Drake being so responsible made some of my tension about them ease...just a little. It wasn't like I was going to get over these feelings overnight. I wanted better things for Lana in life than a rock star. I wanted her to go to college, live it up a little without having to worry about anything else. I wanted her to have the things and chances that I never got. It wasn't me trying to live through her; it was me wanting a better life for her than what I had at her age.

"Tomorrow he's taking Lucy and me shopping." She shook her head. "I told him I didn't want anything, that all I wanted was to spend time with him, but he insisted. He wants to buy me things, Layla. How do I say no to him? I can't..." She trailed off with a frown. "I don't want him to think that the only reason I want to be friends with him is so I can take advantage of the things he can give me. I just want him."

I had no clue how to help her with that. Drake, as far as I could tell, had never been one to splurge on anything. All the pictures I had ever seen of him in tabloids had showed him in tattered old jeans and tee shirts. He never had a woman hanging off his arm, unless you counted Emmie, which I didn't. Maybe his buying Lana things was the only way he knew how to make her see that he cared about her, but I could be wrong.

"Do what you have to do, Lana. When he tries to buy you something, insist that you don't want it." I grasped her hand and gave it a little squeeze. "I'm happy you had a good time, sweetie. Now go shower and get to bed. We can talk in the morning."

She hugged me tight. "He really is a good guy, Layla," she murmured before standing. "You'll see."

I just smiled as I watched her walk into the bedroom. Only time would tell about Drake, but I really hoped that Lana was right.

Jesse

Emmie was much calmer after her talk with Layla. No one wanted to go into the studio on Wednesday, but she insisted. Somehow we made it through the day without losing our minds and actually got two tracks done.

I spent the day with my mind split between worrying about Emmie and how she was handling the news that she was going to have to have a C-section and daydreaming about Layla. By the time we got home that evening, I was anxious to see them both.

Emmie was getting over the distress of the new development where the baby was concerned. She and Nik had talked about it long and hard the night before, and I think that Nik was more worried about it than Em was now. Poor guy had been off most of the day, missing notes, forgetting words that he wrote himself. I felt sorry for him. If it was bothering me so bad, I could only imagine how he had to be feeling. Em was everything to him, and the baby was something that he had grown obsessed with over the summer. His happiness depended on both of them.

THE ROCKER THAT SAVORS ME

Layla had taken off before I got home. I was beyond disappointed. I wanted to knock on her door and invite myself into the guesthouse but decided that it was better to wait. Maybe she needed some space after the kiss the day before.

Drake disappeared every evening after dinner. I was actually jealous of the time he was spending with Lana. I wanted to have the same time with Layla! I wanted to go on long walks with her along the beach. I wanted to lie on a blanket in the grass and just watch the night sky while talking about nothing that really mattered.

Don't get me wrong. I was happy for my buddy. Since Lana had come along, Drake had even slowed down on his drinking. He didn't constantly have a bottle in his hand. He barely drank a beer with dinner each night. Then I would hear him stumbling around in his room in the middle of the night, hear his quiet moans while he fought his nightmares once he finally fell asleep. Just like I heard him throwing up each morning. Something that wasn't a part of his hangover, but the result of his nightmares.

I couldn't think about Drake's nightmares though. They just pissed me off and made me want to punch something.

Friday night he didn't have dinner with us. Emmie said he was going out with Lana, and I wondered if that was a good idea. Emmie seemed thrilled about it, and I trusted her judgment on this, so I didn't say anything.

We were all still up when Drake came home. It wasn't late, barely after eleven. I was relieved when he walked into the house. The look on his face startled me though. He was actually humming, and I had never seen him smiling so freely before the entire time I'd known the guy. Even I would admit that Drake, like his brother, was a sexy fucker, but when he smiled, it shined from the inside out and made him almost beautiful.

Emmie jumped up and hugged him tight. "How was it? Did you have fun?" She sounded like a mother asking her son how his first date went. It wasn't far off the mark. It was probably Drake's first actual date, and she mothered us all.

He laughed and pulled her down on the end of the sectional with him. "It was just dinner, Em."

THE ROCKER THAT SAVORS ME

"I don't care. Tell me all about it."

"Maybe later." He kissed the top of her head, and she snuggled closer to him with a little pout. "No, sweetheart. I can't right now."

"Tomorrow?"

He rolled his eyes at her but was still grinning. "Tomorrow."

I emptied the rest of my beer and got up to throw it away. "I'm calling it a night." I stopped behind Emmie to place a kiss on her cheek. "I finally get to sleep in tomorrow!"

"You get most of next week off, you big baby," Nik grumbled. "So stop complaining."

I shot him the finger. "Not my fault I'm so damn good at what I do that you get the drums down on the first go." I winked down at Emmie. "Night, sweetheart."

"Night, Jesse," she called after me.

I tossed the beer bottle in the recycling can in the kitchen before heading up to my room. Instead of crashing on the bed, I moved to the window. It didn't overlook the beach but the guesthouse. It was dark except for the flashing light of a television in the living room. I imagined Layla lying there on that damned hide-a-bed and wished I was there with her right now.

Layla

I had the whole day to myself. It was something that never happened, but I wasn't going to complain about it. I spent the morning just vegging out in front of the television, watching pure crap. It was stuff that would rot my mind, but I loved every second of it. After a small lunch of cereal and a bagel, I took a long soak in the bathtub and then washed my hair.

Emmie called me on my new cellphone and asked if I wanted to come over to swim, but I was enjoying some me time far too much to want to end it just yet. She seemed a little disappointed, but I promised her that I would spend the entire day with her by the pool the next day, and she cheered up. I loved spending time with Emmie.

THE ROCKER THAT SAVORS ME

Lana and Lucy got home from their day with Drake just after four. Lucy came running into the guesthouse full of excited energy. She was already telling me about her day while Lana stormed into the bedroom and slammed the door behind her. I glanced over at the front door to see Drake glaring after her, his arms loaded with bags of clothes and toys.

"Lucy, go watch some cartoons." I pushed her towards the sofa. "You can tell me all about your day later, I promise."

"Okay." She sighed. "Don't yell at Drake. It isn't his fault that Lana is so rotten."

I shot her a look that told her to keep quiet and moved over to the door where Drake dropped his load of bags on the floor. "How was your day?" I asked.

His jaw tensed and he finally turned his glare from the closed bedroom door to me. Those blue gray eyes of his were gorgeous, the way they were all glassy and full of stormy emotions, even when he was pissed off. "Your sister is so stubborn!" he informed me. As if I didn't already know that! Ha!

I couldn't help but grin. "I'm sure it wasn't that bad."

"She didn't want me to buy her anything. Nothing! Not one little thing. Then when I bought them anyway, she stormed out of the store and left me there with poor little Lucy. She refused to speak to me the rest of the afternoon…" He ran a hand through his long hair and pulled at the roots. "She makes me f…uh…freaking bonkers!"

I admired the way he caught himself from swearing. I had noticed the weekend before that he and the others tried not to swear when Lucy was around. "Give her a little while. She won't stay mad forever. Lana's the type of girl that doesn't want material things. She learned the hard way that people trying to buy her affections didn't exactly mean that they cared about her." I saw his eyes darken as if my words had smacked him in the chest. "She would rather you pick her a flower beside the road than buy her one in a flower shop."

"I wasn't…I just wanted…" He raked his hands through his hair again, looking sick to his stomach. "I'll call her later," he muttered and turned to leave.

THE ROCKER THAT SAVORS ME

I stood in the doorway and watched him make his way back towards the big house. He looked almost defeated with his head bowed and his shoulders slightly slumped. I felt bad for him, but he and Lana had to figure it all out on their own. When he was out of sight, I closed the door and picked up the bags filled with expensive clothes.

My eyes got huge when I saw that they were from an exclusive boutique on Rodeo Drive. I could just imagine the money he had spent there. Leaving Lucy in the living room with a cartoon movie on, I took Lana's new things into the bedroom. She was lying on the king sized bed glaring up at the ceiling.

"Drake said he will call you later," I told her as I dropped the bags on the bed and started snooping through them.

I pulled out jeans with designer labels on them, tops made of silk instead of cotton, and two dresses that made me want to weep they were so beautiful. There were two shoe boxes: one with heels that were to die for in a passion red and another with boots that just begged to be worn by me... Okay, maybe not by me, but if Lana thought I wasn't going to borrow them, she could think again!

"I told him I didn't want anything," Lana muttered. "He said he just wanted me to try a few things on, and I didn't have to get them if I didn't want them. So I tried them on. It was fun but then the sales girl started ringing everything up, and he kept adding more and more things to the pile. I didn't want them. I don't want them! But would he listen to me? No!" She punched the bed beside of her. "I don't want his fucking money. I don't want what he can buy me. I just want to spend time with him!"

"Don't say fuck," I gently admonished her.

"Oh, shut up, Layla," she grumbled. "You say it all the time."

"Yeah, but you're better than me. Don't curse."

"Don't you go starting that again!" Lana sat up, glaring at me now instead of the ceiling. "I'm not better than you. No one is better than you, Layla. You are the best person in the world in my eyes. I don't care about your past or what you had to do to survive when Mom kicked you out. I love you!"

I clenched my jaw, not wanting to think about the past. "So what happened after he bought you the clothes?" I asked, changing the subject back to her day with Drake.

"I walked away. He still bought the clothes. When he and Lucy came out of the store, he drove us to another one that was just for kids and bought Lucy just as many clothes and half a dozen stuffed animals." She shook her head again. "And he got mad at me for being mad at him. Really? He's such a child sometimes! Thirty one years old and he acts younger than Lucy! Pouting because I wouldn't talk to him. Muttering to himself…"

"Oh, Lana! You have that man wrapped so tightly around your finger…" I laughed when she glared at me. "He likes you. And I can see that he cares about you. Give the guy a break. He doesn't know about how you grew up. He doesn't understand your mentality when it comes to things like this. But I told him you aren't like most girls. When he calls, talk to him. Tell him why you don't like gifts, baby."

Her amber eyes closed and she dropped back on the bed again. "I'm not ready to talk about the past. He either accepts that I don't want him buying me things or he doesn't." She turned on her side, away from me. "Problem solved."

I blew out a long sigh. "It isn't always that easy, Lana, but you handle this the way you think you should. Until then, I'm borrowing these kick ass boots to wear tonight."

"You can have it all. I don't want any of it."

THE ROCKER THAT SAVORS ME

Chapter 10
Jesse

Emmie woke me around two. I wasn't expecting the glass of cold water, but I guess I should have. It was the easiest way to wake my ass up. I slept hard and enjoyed every second of it, but try to wake me up and you had a good thirty minute workout unless you tried to drown me.

I sat up in bed, water dripping down my face. "What?" I cried. "What's wrong?"

She stood over my bed in a bikini top and wraparound skirt, her belly sticking out in a cute way that made me want to rub it. The grin on her face told me that she was in a good mood, and it scared the shit out of me. "What are you up to?" I demanded, wiping water off my chest with my damp sheet.

"Nothing." She sat the glass down on the table beside my bed.

"Nothing, my ass." I tossed back the covers and stood. I was naked but she didn't bother to turn around. She didn't bat an eye as she watched me pull out a pair of boxers from my dresser and pull them on. "Where's Nik?"

"Around." She was still grinning and it only made me nervous.

"Around," I repeated, reaching for a pair of jeans from my closet. "Around where?"

"He might be tied up down by the pool with his own shirt." She shrugged as if it wasn't that big of a deal. "But it's his own fault. He invited fucking Axton and the bitch troll over tonight."

I grimaced, pitying my dumb ass friend, and yet I couldn't help but be amused. Nik was going to pay big time if he hadn't already. Emmie and Gabriella Moreitti got along about as well as a king cobra and a mongoose, meaning not at all. I hadn't figured out which was the snake and which was the mongoose, but I was leaning towards Emmie being the mongoose. She could kick Gabriella's ass if she had to.

I wasn't exactly the biggest fan of Gabriella. Maybe it was because she didn't get along with Emmie and I was overprotective. Maybe it was because she had filled Emmie's head with lies about herself and Nik. Or maybe it was because she tended to act like she was better than Emmie. Either way I couldn't have cared less about the bitch. If it weren't for Axton, who was cool to party with, I wouldn't put up with her...even if she could rock hard.

"So are they here? Is that why you woke me up?" I glanced at the clock. It was just past two thirty, and I still had several hours before my date with Layla.

"Not yet." She dropped down on the edge of my bed. "I wanted company. I called Layla but she's enjoying some time to herself. Shane left hours ago for only Gods know where. Probably an orgy or something even more fucked up. And with Nik all tied up..." She snickered at that. "Which left you."

I grinned. "What about Drake? Couldn't you have woke him up and gotten him to keep you company?"

Her green eyes sparkled with joy. "He went out. Took the SUV. It surprised the hell out of me, but he was up before I was. He left me a note saying he was taking Lana and Lucy out shopping and would be back later this evening." She clapped her hands together in glee. It was such an un-Emmie thing to do that it made me laugh. "I'm so happy for him." Drake being up early was a surprise in and of itself, him shopping with two girls, a miracle. The man didn't buy things...ever. I doubt he had even touched any of the money we made over the last ten years. Emmie bought him clothes when she thought he had worn out the ones he had and bought his personal items, even down to his condoms. I was glad for Drake, really, and thrilled that he seemed so happy with Lana around. But..."Em, is this really okay?" I couldn't help but ask. "Could Drake be in over his head here? She's only seventeen. And while I trust him wholeheartedly with the girl, I'm worried that he's feeling way too much, way too soon."

"I always knew that when Drake found the right girl, it would change everything." She sighed, gently rubbing a hand over that basketball stomach of hers. "I will admit that I wasn't expecting her to be so young. But I'm not going to look this gift horse in the mouth, Jesse. Besides, it's still in its early stages. We don't even know if she's what he needs. Right now, I'm just happy that he's happy."

THE ROCKER THAT SAVORS ME

I rubbed a hand over my face, feeling the stubble that needed shaved before I picked up Layla. "Em…About Layla…" I needed her approval. It was weird, really. I shouldn't need anyone's opinion on who I dated, but Emmie's opinion was the only one that mattered to me. If I didn't get it, I didn't think that would stop me from going after Layla, not with how strongly I felt towards her. Without her approval it could make the whole thing feel wrong in a way.

Another sigh left her. "I really like her, Jess. Please, don't hurt her. Okay? I mean, I can see that there is something between you two. And if I had to choose, you know you will always be the one I pick, but she's become my friend, and I don't want to lose that. Just be careful."

I nodded. "I promise, Em." I pressed a kiss to her cheek and then stood. "Come on. I bet Nik is going apeshit down there. You really are a twisted little bitch, you know that?"

She laughed. "Yeah, I know."

I found Nik lying on a lounger with nothing on but a pair of swimming trunks. His arms were tied to the lounger with his shirt while he glared up at me. "I'm going to spank her. I should have done it years ago. You just wait. As soon as I'm free, she's going to get my hand print on that sweet ass of hers."

Instead of untying him, I sat down on the lounger across from him. "Well now. See, I was going to help you out, man. But you threatening my Emmie like that just got you a few more minutes."

Emmie stuck her tongue out at him as she dropped down beside me and cuddled close. "See. Told you he would be on my side." Her stomach pressed against my side, and she laid her head on my chest. "Better treat me better, mister."

"Ah, fuck. Come on, Emmie!" He twisted on the lounger, but his shirt was tied in a knot that I had taught Emmie myself so I knew he wasn't getting loose anytime soon. "Alright, I'm sorry. I should have known better than to invite Ax over with Brie…Gabriella," he amended when she gave him a killing glare. "Baby, please. I'll fix it. I swear… If you love me, you will untie me, Em!"

THE ROCKER THAT SAVORS ME

"You know I love you, Nikolas Armstrong," she told him but went back to cuddling close to me. "Too bad you haven't shown me you love me today."

Nik went still on the lounger. Emmie had gotten a direct hit on him and shit was about to get real. I closed my eyes, savoring my time with Em, before Nik took her away. A minute later, a large shadow landed over us and I opened my eyes to see Nik. His arms were still tied behind his back, but somehow he had gotten free of the lounger. Without a word, he turned and I untied him.

As soon as his hands were free, he lifted Emmie into his arms. His blue eyes were darker than I had ever seen them. Anger and hurt seemed to pour from him. "I think we need to have a long talk, Ember."

"Nik...I was just kidding." Emmie clutched at his shoulders as he turned on his heel and stalked into the house with her still in his arms. "Nik!"

"Shut up, Em," he snapped and kept on walking.

I knew that he wouldn't hurt her, but I had to follow them inside. He hadn't gone far. I stopped outside of the living room where Nik had put her on the long end of the sectional and stood glaring down at her. His hands raked through his hair, making him look slightly demented.

"Do I not show you how much I love you every day, Em?" he demanded.

Emmie sighed. "Of course you do. Look, I'm sorry. It was just a joke."

"Well don't fucking joke around about that! I love you, baby. You are my everything. If you don't believe me, then tell me now so I can fix it." He fell to his knees in front of her. "Tell me, Em."

"I know that you love me. It took me a little while, but I really believe you. I'm sorry I said that, Nik." I heard the tears in her voice now and had to restrain my urge to pound my friend in the face. Emmie should never cry. Never! "I was being a bitch and I'm sorry. I get a little evil like that when I think of you and Gabriella in the same room."

"Em, I told you nothing happened. She lied to you. Gabriella is nothing to me. Nothing! It was always you and she used that to hurt you." Nik pulled her into his arms and kissed her tenderly. "Please believe me, baby."

"I...I...believe you."

I turned away, feeling as if I was intruding. Nik and Emmie had come a long way over the summer. Sometimes Em had moments when she second guessed Nik's feelings, but they worked through their problems. Nik had his hands full with her insecurities, but he never lost his patience when it came to showing Em what she meant to him.

I kind of wanted what they had, insecurities and all.

Layla

I left Lana and Lucy in front of the television with a large cheese pizza. Lana was still stuck between pouting and glaring off into space. I hoped that she and Drake would be able to sort it out before I got home. Sure, Lana was over reacting a little about Drake buying her things, but her life had been full of the men our mother had paraded before her, all trying to win her over with expensive things so they could get closer to Lydia...or the really perverted ones trying to get closer to her!

Been there done that. It was why my mother had thrown me out when I was sixteen. One of her boyfriends had taken a sick liking to me, and one night he had tried to climb into bed with me. When I had woken up to a naked forty year old man beside me, I freaked out. I screamed until everyone in the house was up. My mother had taken one look at the picture—me only in my night gown, her boyfriend naked and in my bed—and went ballistic. She pulled me up out of my bed and dragged me out of the house. I wasn't sure what had happened to the boyfriend, but I did know that Lydia had considered the whole thing my fault. She was insecure about her age, hated that she was getting older and losing the fresh young looks that she had always relied on to help find sugar daddies—and rock stars—to pay her bills for her. It hadn't mattered to her that I was only sixteen. All she had cared about was that I was prettier than she was and therefore competition.

If she hadn't died when she did, I was sure she would have ended up tossing Lana out too. Lana, who was so much more beautiful than I was, would have been serious trouble for Lydia's self-esteem.

At seven, there was a knock on the front door, and my heart moved to my throat. It was crazy that I was nervous. It wasn't like this was my first date or anything. I had boyfriends in the past and even thought I was in love a time or two, but this was different. Jesse was different.

When I opened the door, the sight before me took my breath away. Dressed in jeans, a shirt that stretched across that massive chest, and biker boots, he was my version of sexy multiplied by ten. Screw the date! I wanted to haul him into the closest bed and devour him whole.

His eyes changed colors as soon as he saw me, Going dark and animalistic as he trailed his gaze from the top of my head to my toes. I had left my hair down with the ends just slightly curled to add some body. My makeup wasn't all that special except I had paid extra attention to my eye makeup, giving them a smoky look with cool grays and metallic blues. His eyes paused momentarily on my chest, obviously liking the way my top clung to my breast. The skinny jeans I had on were a pair of Lana's, and they tightly hugged my hips. The boots that Drake had bought her finished my look, and I could almost see the fantasies Jesse was having in his eyes—imagining me with nothing but those boots on.

He rubbed a hand over his mouth, taking his time as his eyes made the return trip back up to my face. "Killing me here, baby."

I grinned, loving that I was affecting him so much. "I can change."

"No." He shook his head and grasped my hand. "I like that you are killing me." He tugged me out the door, and I called a "good night" to the girls before shutting the door behind us.

I had never had someone open a car door for me and really wasn't expecting it from the big bad rocker, but he surprised me when he did just that. Stopping by the SUV, he opened the door and didn't let go of my hand until I was seated in the passenger seat. As he closed the door, another vehicle pulled up beside of the Escalade.

THE ROCKER THAT SAVORS ME

I didn't pay attention to who was in the Ferrari because I was too busy checking out the car itself. In the dim lighting, I saw that it was metallic silver. The art work on the driver's side was *sick* with skulls in black and dark shades of gray. I was instantly in love with the car!

Jesse called a greeting to the couple getting out of the car but didn't stop as he moved around to climb behind the wheel of the Escalade. I caught a glimpse of long dark hair from a woman shorter than I was and the tattoos on the arms of the man as they walked up the steps to the front door. I saw for the first time just who it was... "Is that Axton Cage?"

Jesse glanced back at the beach house as the door opened and Nik stood in the door way. "Yeah... Did you want to meet him? We have time."

I shook my head. It would have been cool to have met the man deemed "Rock God," but I was more excited to just be with the rocker beside me. "I'd rather be with you," I told him honestly.

His hand stopped in the process of starting the vehicle. Eyes darker than I had ever seen captured mine, and before I could blink he was reaching for me. I went willingly, desperate for the taste of him. He wasn't gentle and it only served to make me want more. His tongue thrusting into my mouth made me wet, and I nearly climbed across the seat to straddle him.

He tasted like toothpaste with something more potent underlying that mint flavor. That something went straight to my head, and I became an instant addict for it. A small moan escaped my mouth, and I clutched his shoulders, my nails sinking into his flesh through the material of his shirt.

The kiss went on and on. It could have lasted hours and I wouldn't have been able to get my fill. When he finally raised his head, it was because we needed to breathe. He leaned his forehead against mine, his fingers tangling in my hair to hold me close. "Seriously, Layla. Killing me here, baby."

I bit my lip to stop myself from attacking his mouth again. "I'm dying a little myself," I whispered.

We sat there for several minutes. It was soothing the way his fingers, still tangled in my hair, massaged my scalp while we got

THE ROCKER THAT SAVORS ME

our breathing under control. When he raised his head, his eyes had changed again. They weren't as dark as they had been just a few minutes ago, but they weren't his normal brown. He pressed a kiss to my forehead before turning in the seat and reaching out to start the SUV.

"What would you like to eat, babe? Italian, Greek, Mexican?" He reversed, backing smoothly out of the driveway. "Anything you want just let me know."

I told him I wanted a hamburger, and he just blinked at me. "Really?"

I grinned. "Yes, really. But I want a really good hamburger. The best hamburger in the world. Know a place like that?"

"Yeah, but it's in New York." He frowned as if thinking about his options then turned left at a red light. "Okay. I know a good place. It isn't the best burger you will ever eat, but it is as close as I can get without flying across the country."

He took me to a little mom-and-pop place that was surprisingly crowded. We seated ourselves in the back at a little booth, and a waitress in her late thirties came to take our orders. She barely gave us a once over before asking us what we wanted to drink. Two cokes and two full works burgers later and we were both stuffed, of course Jesse had finished my burger because it had been so huge that I had only been able to eat half. The man could eat because not only did he have his burger and mine, but he ate most of the fries that had come with both as well.

Even though I had only eaten half, it was still the best burger I had ever had. I didn't know if it was because of the food or because of the company I had while I enjoyed it. Jesse kept me laughing through our meal—telling me all kinds of hilarious things about him and the band over the years—and I felt lighthearted by the time he paid the bill.

He stood and captured my hand as soon as I was on my feet. It felt right when he entwined our fingers and pulled me close as we walked out of the restaurant. The parking lot was crowded with more cars coming and going. It was dark out now, and there were only a few street lights to guide us to the Escalade, but I wasn't scared; there was no one in the world stupid enough to mess with

Jesse. It made me feel safe because he was so big and almost scary looking in the dim lighting.

He opened the passenger door for me, but when I went to step up into the big SUV, he stopped me with a firm hand on my waist. All too willingly, I melted into his arms as his head lowered and caught my mouth. My arms snaked around his shoulders so I could hold on while I pulled myself up his body enough to feel his cock right where I needed it the most.

I was already wet and aching for this man. His kisses made me weak in the knees, and I felt as if I was coming undone with each second that passed while his mouth tortured me with the addictive taste of him. He groaned low in his throat when I moved so his cock was pressed against my pussy. "Fuck, Layla," he muttered, his lips trailing down my neck and nipping at my shoulder. "Why is it that as soon as your lips touch mine, I'm ready to come in my jeans?"

"I'd rather you come in me," I whispered brokenly and his fingers tightened their hold on my waist to the point of pain.

"I want to take you right here." He sucked at the spot he had nipped, tenderly making blood pool at the surface. "But I'm not going to..." I whimpered in protest. I wasn't one for public sex, but I was willing to make an exception for this man! "I promised you a date, and the night is still young, baby." He raised his head and dark eyes captured mine. "But later..."

Jesse

If I knew that our night was going to end the way it did, I would have taken her home and sunk my dick into her as soon as I had paid for dinner. Hind sight was always twenty/twenty...

I parked the Escalade in the parking lot across the road from the bar. Every time the door opened, loud music poured out. The band wasn't due to preform until ten, so we still had an hour or so before they took the stage. For now, there was a DJ in the back playing good rock and everyone was having a good time.

The bouncer at the door barely looked at our IDs when I paid the cover charge, and then I caught hold of Layla's hand and pulled her through the crowd towards the bar. It was so loud that I had to press my lips to her ear so she could hear me. She shivered when I asked her what she wanted to drink.

Layla shrugged. "What are you having?" she asked.

"Let's do some shots. You cool with that?" She nodded her head in agreement. Luckily enough, two guys were just leaving their chairs at the bar when we approached, and I lifted Layla into one before waving at the bartender.

A skinny guy with a long goatee raised a brow at me when he stopped in front of us. "What do you want Layla? Jack Daniels or Patron?"

"Patron. Jack gives me a headache." The guy sat two shot glasses in front of us and poured our shots then added a slice of lime to each and put a salt shaker beside the glasses. I gave him a fifty and told him to keep the change.

Before I could reach for mine, Layla already swallowed her own. I watched in fascination as she swallowed without so much as flinching and bit into the lime without bothering with the salt. Fuck me! My dick, which had been on the verge of exploding all evening, twitched against the fly of my jeans, and I quickly swallowed my shot before I did something stupid, like pull her into the bathroom in the back and screw her brains out.

But that wasn't how it was going to be the first time we made love. It was going to be in a bed, and I was going to take my time with her. There was no use in rushing, not with Layla. She was different from any other woman that had warmed my bed. I felt it in my bones when I looked at her.

The heat of the tequila distracted me enough to get my cock under control for the moment, and I motioned to the bartender for two more. Layla gave me a sly grin as she downed the second shot without bothering with the lime this time. I placed a kiss on her lips just to get a taste of her and found that she was far more intoxicating than the liquor.

Big chocolate eyes blinked up at me as I drew back a little. "Not fair, rock star."

I laughed, completely and utterly happy in that moment. "Nothing about the way you make me feel is fair, Layla," I assured her.

THE ROCKER THAT SAVORS ME

"Evil man," she grumbled with a grin.

The skinny guy stopped in front of us again. "Layla?" She shrugged and I switched us from shots of Patron to rum and coke. I didn't want us completely wasted, just buzzed enough to enjoy ourselves for a few hours. When I left I wanted her sober and completely in control of herself so she could say no to me if that was what she really wanted. I prayed to every god I knew of that she wouldn't say no to me!

We sat there sipping our drinks for a long while. The bar was getting pretty crowded. All walks of life were in attendance: college kids, a few bikers, Goths, and Emos. I didn't feel out of place like the preppies that were huddled in the back at a table. Everyone gave them a wide berth because they were loud and starting to get obnoxious.

When the band came out on stage, everyone moved closer. Nik had asked me to take a look at them because Rich had mentioned something about them to him. They had gotten popular over the summer because of something on YouTube, and Rich was thinking of signing them and putting them as our opening act when we eventually started touring again.

Layla, who was now sipping on a Vodka and Cranberry, stood in front of me. I kept an arm around her waist, needing to touch her at all times. It wasn't because I felt like she wasn't safe; I just needed the contact. When the band started their intro, she pressed her rear right into my crotch, and my mind went completely blank for a full minute.

Around us, people were going crazy for the band, and I finally snapped out of my desire filled fog. I pressed a kiss just under Layla's ear. "Careful, baby. Any more of that and I won't be able to walk out of here."

I couldn't hear her laugh, but I felt it vibrating through her and into me.

When I was able to focus on the band on stage I found that they were mostly a cover band. They didn't have anything original to offer, but they were pretty good at the rock songs that they covered. The guitarist could have kept up with Drake, and that was saying something because Drake was king when it came to playing with strings. The frontrunner had a kind of raspy voice that made people stop and take notice, but he lacked a certain personality that lead singers needed for a performance. I liked the drummer's skills, but the guy on bass was off by a cord or two from time to time.

All in all, it was a great band to see at a bar, but I wasn't all that sure if they were what Rich was looking for. And I was in serious doubt of Nik agreeing to let them open for us if Rich really did sign them. If Rich brought them on board there would have to be some major changes within the band itself.

Still, they were cool to listen to tonight. Layla seemed to be having a good time as they continued to play some really good rock songs. The liquor had loosened her up, and she was dancing in front of me now. With her hair whipping around as she moved that sexy little body so provocatively, I fought with myself over hauling her out of the bar right then and there. I wasn't the only one enjoying the sight of Layla dancing. Several guys around us had turned their attention from the band to her as she moved her ass to the beat. Even as my dick reacted to her, my rage boiled as a guy from the preppy table dared to approach her.

I had lost my hold on her waist a few songs ago to give her free rein to dance to her heart's content. She had moved a few feet away from me, and I had been cool with that, but now Preppy with the light pink polo and gelled hair was taking advantage of the distance between us.

I watched it as if in slow motion as the guy pressed up against her side and she leaned into him for half a second before she realized that the man touching her was not me. She stepped back, glaring up at Preppy, but he pulled her back into his arms and started grinding his hips against her.

Maybe it wouldn't have bothered me so much if she hadn't been trying to get away from the douche bag, but she was pushing against his chest and he wouldn't let her go. Okay, it wasn't just because of that. Layla was mine and no one, absolutely no one, touched what was mine!

Two steps forward and I was beside Layla. She looked up at me in relief until she saw the fire in my eyes. "Jesse..." she started, but I didn't give her time to finish her sentence as I pushed between her and Preppy.

The guy was a tool—the kind that did nothing but worry about how good he looked. He probably spent hours at the gym to get his abs just right, had a hundred dollars' worth of product in his slightly spiked hair. His clothes were from Hollister, and I was almost positive that he was the kind of guy that thought he could have anything and everything handed to him with just a snap of his fingers.

Well, he wasn't fucking getting my girl!

"What's up dude?" the guy shouted up at me, taking a step back when I got between him and Layla. "I'm dancing here."

My eyes narrowed. "Dance somewhere else."

Layla pressed up against my back, her hands rubbing at my shoulders in an attempt to make me relax. "Jess, it's okay. Dance with me and forget about him."

I might have done just that if Preppy hadn't opened his mouth again. "Sorry, dude. Didn't know she was taken for the night. That's one fine piece of ass you got…" He didn't finish what he was going to say. He couldn't. Not when my fist practically broke his jaw and he fell on his ass in the middle of the bar.

His friends, all six of them, rushed over to help him to his feet. All of them seemed to be as clueless as he was because the one in the middle tried to jump on me. Like Preppy, this guy was just as much a tool as the rest. He swung his fist, directed at my chin, but I was quicker than him. Years of drumming gave me faster reflexes than most people. I stepped back causing the guy to fall on his face with the force he had put behind his punch.

"Jesse!" Layla called a warning as two more jumped to the aid of their fallen friends.

Bouncers were pushing through the crowd to get to us, but I didn't bother to wait for them. My fist connected with the first's stomach causing the air to rush from his body, and he bent in half trying to suck in oxygen. The second got a cheap shot, and his fist connected with the side of my face. It hurt like hell, but it only made me angrier. I grabbed him by his expensive shirt and lifted him a few inches off the ground. "Your mistake," I growled at him.

Our tussle had caught everyone's attention, and even the band had stopped playing now. I heard someone shout out my name, "That's Jesse Thornton!" I ignored them as I slung the guy I still had a hold of on to the floor and bent down to punch him in the face.

"Jesse..." Layla tried to catch my attention. The rest of the group was attempting to get their friends on their feet.

Four bouncers finally broke through the crowd that had surrounded us. One stepped towards me, but Layla got between them and me. "It wasn't his fault," she defended me. "That guy..." she pointed to Preppy "...he was manhandling me. Jesse was just protecting me. Then these guys..." She pointed to the three that were still on the ground, two of them groaning. "Tried to jump him. He was just defending himself."

"Layla?" One of the other bouncers stepped forward and frowned at Layla.

She stiffened when the guy came closer. "Oh. Hey, Kyle..." She gave him a small, tight smile. Her reaction made me take a closer look at the bouncer. Not quite six feet with some well-defined muscles, he had a chip in one of his front teeth and a scar just above his left eye.

He wasn't much to look at, but the way he was looking at Layla made me think that he had seen her without her clothes on. That thought alone made me take a threatening step towards the guy. Layla's arms wrapped around my waist to stop me. "No," she whispered. "Calm down."

I took a few deep breaths in an attempt to calm my rage. She sighed and turned enough so she was facing the bouncers again. "We were just trying to have a good time, Kyle. These guys started the fight."

"It's fine, Layla," Kyle told her. "This lot has been causing trouble left and right all night long. You and Thornton go back to enjoying your evening." They pushed the preppies to their feet and out the door. "It was good seeing you. Call me sometime."

"Umm...sure," she murmured as the bouncers walked away and everyone around us tried to act like nothing had happened. The band started up where they had left off, and I had to give them points for playing it cool like that.

"Friend of yours?" I couldn't help asking as I glared after the bouncer named Kyle.

She snorted. "Kyle? No. He was the bouncer at the club I used to work at a few years ago." She grimaced. "But that was a life time ago."

I pulled her closer, burying my face in her hair as I tried to get my rage under complete control. I hadn't gotten into a fight like that in a long time, but I'd never fought over a girl before. I wasn't the jealous type, at least not normally, but there was nothing normal about what I felt for Layla.

She held me until the rage seeped from my body, her fingers tracing soothing patterns on my back under my shirt. Her sweet scent filled my nose, and my body grew tense for another reason all together. "How about another drink?" she offered.

"Yeah, I think we need one." I kissed her lips quick and hard then pulled her towards the bar.

Chapter 11
Layla

We weren't back at the bar five minutes before three guys approached Jesse. They were obviously fans. Jesse was good-natured about signing autographs, but after a few minutes of conversation, he excused us. "Sorry, guys. I'm here with my girl." He pulled me against his chest.

The guys gave him knowing grins and left us alone. I took a long pull from my beer and wrapped myself around him. "I'm sorry," I told him.

He frowned down at me. "What the hell are you sorry for?" he demanded. "I'm the one who's sorry. I ruined our first date."

"No. I shouldn't have been dancing like that." I should have known better than to even start, but I had been having so much fun and the music was pretty good. I had felt safe knowing that Jesse was right behind me, and I wanted to dance just for him, feeling his eyes burning into my back while I moved to the music. I had gotten carried away and attracted more attention than I had wanted.

"Layla, you can dance however you fucking like, whenever you like. That douche bag was just asking for trouble. Everyone in this place knew you were with me. He was drunk and thought he owned the world, you included. I shouldn't have let him get to me, but I wasn't going to let him talk about you like that." He grasped my hand and brought my fingers to his lips. "Let's not let him and his friends ruin the rest of our night. Okay, baby?"

I smiled, equal parts of heart melting and panty melting as he nibbled on my fingers. "I promise not to if you promise not to."

"Deal." He ordered us each a beer and then pulled me to the back of the bar so we could listen to the band. There were no seats left at the bar, but I didn't want to sit. He leaned back against the wall and pulled me into his arms before giving me one of the beers.

The band was playing a slower song now, and I snuggled closer to him. His hand slipped over my hip and stayed there while his fingers beat a soft rhythm to the music. Jesse's lips were close to my ear, and I could hear him humming along to the song. I was content to stand there in his strong arms while we drank our beers. It felt good... It felt right.

When his beer was gone, he pulled me in front of him so my back was to his chest. Those muscled arms of his wrapped around my waist, and I turned my head to smile at him over my shoulder when I felt his erection twitching against my ass. He buried his nose in my hair, and I pulled it over my right shoulder so he could kiss my neck instead.

His tongue skimmed over my exposed flesh, causing goose bumps to rise and me to shiver. "Jesse." I sighed and pressed my rear into him.

"Can we get out of here?" He breathed against the shell of my ear.

I pouted up at him. "I don't want to go home." I wasn't ready to tell him goodnight. I wanted... Fuck, I wanted so many things! We could do any of them if he took me home. There was no way I was having sex with him in the guesthouse, not when my sisters were there, and I didn't think I could look at myself in the morning if he took me to the beach house. I didn't want everyone to know what I sounded like when I was coming apart for this man.

A wicked, hot tongue slipped inside my ear, and I nearly came then and there. "Not going home tonight, baby. Will you come with me?"

I had no choice. I wanted—shit, I needed this man! Unable to speak I was so messed up from that kiss to my ear, I simply nodded. His arms tightened around me for a moment before he released me and entwined our fingers. "You won't regret it." He pressed a kiss to my neck then pulled me towards the exit just a few feet away.

The bouncer at the door nodded his head at Jesse as we went out the door, and Jesse was already pulling out his keys to the SUV. I practically ran to keep up with his bigger steps. The air was cooler than when we had first arrived, but I was so hot for him that I barely felt the bite of the late night air. When we reached the SUV, he opened my door and lifted me into the Escalade. His hands lingered on my hips a moment longer than necessary before he stepped back and shut the door.

When he was behind the wheel, he didn't hesitate to pull out into traffic and head for Beverly Hills instead of Malibu. I didn't question where we were going. Neither of us spoke as he reached for my hand and entwined our fingers while he drove through the darkened streets of LA. That contact alone kept me on the edge of a complete melt down. My panties were drenched. My nipple rings rubbed against the material of my bra, keeping me close to an almost panting state. If I crossed my legs just right, I would have cum without him ever having to touch me.

Sometime later, he pulled up in front of a gated mansion and punched in a code that had the gates opening automatically. Moments later, he was parked in front of a house ten times bigger than the beach house. I frowned up at the monstrous sized house. "Jesse, who lives here?"

"A friend of mine. He's out of the country right now." He reached for me, his fingers tangling in my hair as he pulled me close. "I want to make love to you, Layla. Not in some hotel room…and not in my room at the beach house. Not this first time." His lips grazed across mine tenderly. "Say no and I will take you home. It's your choice…but I'm praying that you won't say no."

He knew what my answer was. He had known it on Tuesday when he asked me out for tonight. I wanted him too much to say no. "Your friend won't mind us being here while he's gone?"

"No. I've never done this before, but I've always had an open invitation. Tom is cool with it." He pulled the keys from the ignition and lifted a key from it that had a skull on the base. "When we first got to LA more than ten years ago, we stayed with Tom for a while. He's like the dad none of us ever had, but don't ever tell him that. He has this thing about being called Dad."

I grinned at him. "My lips are sealed." He dropped a quick, hard kiss on my lips and then got out. Before I could even think to follow him, he was around the hood and opening my door. Jesse pulled me out, and we practically ran up the steps to the house.

He fumbled with the lock for a minute before it unlocked. It was dark inside, but Jesse seemed to know the layout of the place well because he didn't even bother to turn on a light as he shut the door behind us, made sure it was locked, and pulled me towards the stairs. "No one's here," he told me. "Not even the housekeeper. When Tom's overseas, he gives her paid vacations. She's the happiest housekeeper in the state. Don't tell Em I told you that."

I laughed. "It's alright. I'm sure that in a few minutes I'll be the happiest housekeeper in the state."

"Oh, fuck yeah." He stopped halfway up the stairs and pressed me against the wall. His dick flexed against me. "I can promise you that much, baby."

With trembling fingers, I pushed him away. "We need a bed, Jesse. Right now."

His eyes turned dark and animalistic. He growled low in his throat as he lifted me over his shoulder. I screamed, laughing as he carried me fireman style up the rest of the stairs and down a long hallway. At the end of the hall, he opened a door. Moments later, I was flying as he tossed me into the middle of a king sized bed. A small lamp came on beside the bed, and I didn't bother to look around the room as he practically tore his shirt off and crawled towards me.

In the dim lighting, he looked more animal than man, and it was the sexiest thing I had ever seen. His muscles flexed with every move he made towards me, and I found myself panting with desperate need for him. "I've never been this turned on in my life," I told him quietly. "And you haven't even touched me yet."

He stopped when he was between my spread thighs. "I'm pretty far gone, Layla. The first time might not be perfect, but I swear to God, I'll make it up to you."

I rolled my eyes. "Baby, you could breathe on my clit and I would come right now. Don't worry about me." I sat up and pulled my top over my head. He sucked in a loud breath when he saw my zebra print bra and the way my nipples pressed against it. When I reached my arms behind me to undo the clasp, he stopped me.

"Let me." Instead of reaching for my bra, he lowered his head and kissed me. He tasted of the beer we drank before leaving the bar, but I could still taste the powerfully addictive taste that was completely Jesse underneath. Any buzz I had had earlier had disappeared on the drive here, but with that innocent taste of him, I was drunk on Jesse.

I sucked his tongue into my mouth, keeping it hostage as I got my fill of him. I didn't think I could ever get enough of this man's taste. I barely noticed when his fingers pulled down the straps of my bra I was so lost in our kiss. Cool air caressed my already hard nipples as they were exposed, making them throb as his chest pressed into mine. I let my fingernails rake over his smooth head, loving the feel of his soft skin under my fingertips.

"Did I ever tell you that bald guys are my kryptonite?" I breathed against his ear while he trailed kisses down my neck.

I felt him grin against my collar bone. "No... Did I ever tell you that you're the most beautiful thing I've ever seen?" He raised his head, the smile gone. "Because you are, Layla."

My heart melted, turning to goo in my chest as I looked up at him through my lashes. "I didn't take you as the romantic type, rock star."

"There's a first time for everything, baby." He winked as he reached behind me and undid my bra with barely any movement of his fingers.

The cups of my bra fell forward, leaving me naked from the waist up. His already dark eyes turned almost black as he took in the little hoops through each of my nipples. "Fuck, that's hot," he muttered.

When he just continued to stare down at me, eating up the sight of my breasts while I ached for his touch, I cupped one of my breast in my hand. My fingers tugged on the little silver hoop, and I cried out in pleasure. "Touch me, Jesse," I whimpered as I cupped my other breast, offering it up to him.

But he shook his head. "I'm about to cum in my jeans, sweetheart. If I touch you, I'm going to seriously embarrass myself."

His honesty was my undoing. I reached between us and carefully undid his top button and unzipped his fly. "Layla..." He started to protest but I leaned forward and brushed a quick, soft kiss across his lips.

"Let me take care of you," I whispered against his lips before pulling back. He was tense, but he let me press him back onto the mattress. He lifted his hips as I tugged at his jeans and didn't hesitate when I pulled off his socks.

When he was completely naked, laid bare before me, I had to stop for a moment and take in the glorious sight that was Jesse Thornton. His eyes, still able to fascinate me with their ever changing colors, were even darker now, and I wondered how dark they would be when he came for me. There was a tattoo on his left peck, just a small one right over his heart. I hadn't given it much thought before, but now that I could inspect it, I saw that it said "Emmie" in delicate cursive. "She is one special girl," I whispered as I dropped a kiss over the name.

"She's the first girl to ever love me unconditionally," Jesse told me as if he was explaining something important to me.

"Then she's the smartest girl I've ever met." As soon as the words left my mouth, I bit my lip. I needed to shut up and now. I was feeling way too emotional about this man, and I needed to get away from all the softer feelings I was having. Time to get this back to what it really was.

My gaze quickly moved from his chest, down that hard angled stomach, and finally lower...

"Fuck!" I couldn't help but exclaim when I saw his dick for the first time. I had been keeping my eyes from that part of his body on purpose until now, but I wished I had looked there first.

Never had I thought of the male genitalia as beautiful before, but this man was perfection. It lifted from his groin proudly, and I had to ball my hands into fists to keep from reaching out to touch it instantly. He was long, longer than I had ever seen, and thick. I doubted both my hands would completely circle his engorged shaft. For just a second, I was nervous because I knew that it wasn't going to be easy to take him the first time.

As I continued to look down at his cock, with the bulging veins and mushroomed head, a tear leaked from the tip. I was unable to continue to sit there and not touch him. I grasped the base with both hands. It was silk poured over hot steel. I stroked my hands up until more of his pre-cum leaked from the tip and lowered my head to lick away the evidence of his need for me.

Jesse tensed even more under me. His hands clenching in the comforter under him. "You're fucking killing me!" he cried out.

I felt powerful. This man, who had been with countless other women, was mine right now. I held the key to his pleasure, at least for the moment, and I was going to wield my power to its full potential.

My tongue swirled around the head. Once. Twice. The third time I took him into my mouth as far as I could and moaned in delight as he hit the back of my throat. His taste burst on my tongue making me moan at the delicious musky flavor. His wide girth stretched my mouth, and I had to take a second to get the rhythm perfect so I'd be able to breathe through my nose.

Jesse's fingers tangled in my hair, tugging at the roots while he cursed. "I fucking love your mouth!" he cried out. I looked up at him through my lashes on each upward movement. He held my hair to the side so he could watch.

"Do you like sucking my dick, Layla?" he demanded.

I moaned my answer, the vibrations from the small noise making his eyes roll back in his head. I cupped his balls, tugging on them gently to extend the pleasure, keeping him from coming when I felt them tighten up. I took him in deeper, his head going down the back of my throat with each thrust into my mouth. Still I wasn't taking all of him and I used my free hand to stroke him.

"Fuck!" He roared and I felt the first jet of semen as it gushed down my throat. I gripped his dick with both hands, stroking him through his orgasm while I swallowed every drop of his hot cum. "Oh, fuck!" He cried again and tried to tug my head away. But I was greedy and wanted ever last drop he could give me.

When I had swallowed the last of it I still sucked on him. He hadn't gotten soft and I thrilled at his ability to go again.

"Enough!" He pulled me away and I fell onto the bed beside of him, reaching for my belt.

I kicked the boots off, and they went flying across the room somewhere. When the belt was undone I shimmed out of the jeans taking the panties with them. I was soaking wet. The scent of my arousal hitting me as soon as my pants were down. Jesse groaned, turning onto his side and propping his head in his hand so he could look down at me.

"You smell amazing." He growled, his free hand cupping my pussy. His thumb skimmed across my clit. "You're dripping for me."

"Yes." I was just able to answer him, my breaths coming in choppy little pants. I arched my hips up, silently begging him to touch me again.

He didn't make me wait. Jesse got up on his knees and moved between my spread thighs. His cock, still damp from my mouth swayed back and forward with each movement and I found myself wanting to taste him again…All thoughts of his cock vanished when he spread the outer lips of my pussy to get a better look at my clit.

"I love your pussy." He murmured. While he kept my lips spread with the fingers of one hand he used the other to skim over my throbbing clit.

My entire body jerked when he flicked at the ball of nerves. "Like that?" He questioned and I could do nothing more than nod. I licked my lips, anticipating his next move. Catching the tender flesh between his thumb and forefinger he twisted it to the left and I cried out in sweet agony. When he twisted it back to the right I begged him to finish me. "Not until I get a taste of that sweet smelling pussy." He growled.

I wasn't going to survive this night! I was sure of it. When his tongue touched my clit, my back arched off the bed and I thought I was going to break in two from the force behind the pleasure. Strong hands gripped my hips, holding me still while he sucked my clit into his mouth, making little popping sounds each time he let it go and then sucking it back in.

Tears poured from my eyes. "Feels so good." I sobbed.

"Best tasting pussy I've ever had." He muttered as he thrust a finger inside of me while he continued to kill me slowly with his tongue.

"Ah. Ah. Ah." My head tossed from side to side, while I tried to press my pussy down harder on his sucking mouth. "Please! Ah!"

Another finger joined the first and he thrust them in and out hard, but not fast like I so desperately needed. "Going to make you come so fucking hard, baby." Jesse promised. "You taste so sweet."

"Oh…Oh!" I couldn't take much more. I was going out of my mind, hanging so close to the edge of an orgasm that was going to be harder than any I had ever experienced before. "Ah!" I twisted the piercings in my nipples trying to push myself over the edge.

"I know." He bit my clit, making me beg for more. "I know it feels so good that you don't want it to end. But I swear to you, sweet Layla. As soon as you come for me I will take you. I will shove my dick in you and fuck you as hard as you want."

His words pulled me down off the edge. I screamed his name over and over again, my fingers sliding over his head to hold him against my gushing pussy while he lapped up every drop of cream that flowed from me. When my inner muscles stopped their relentless spasms he raised his head, a few drops of my thick cum clinging to his lips.

I watched in complete and utter fascination, my breaths coming in shallow pants, as he licked it away. His dark eyes closed, savoring the taste of me on his wicked tongue. It was so incredibly sexy to witness and even though I had just had the most powerful orgasm of my life I burned for him again.

"You promised." I whimpered and his eyes snapped open. "Jess I need you."

Muttering a curse he reached for his jeans and pulled his wallet from the back pocket. His fingers were actually trembling as he ripped open the condom wrapper and rolled it over his thick tip. He pressed the head of his dick against my still quivering pussy and I felt a moment of nervous excitement as he slowly entered me.

He was so thick that he stretched my inner muscles. I have never felt so full. It burned, but there was no real pain. When he was half way in he had to stop, sweat beading on his forehead and upper lip. "Damn, you are so fucking tight."

I swallowed hard. "It's been a while for me."

THE ROCKER THAT SAVORS ME

"Ah, shit!" He closed his eyes, gently rocking back and forward until he was completely in me. "Baby, I'm a wreck! I am going to destroy your beautiful pussy. I can't stop myself."

"Do it." I begged. "I need you to fuck me hard."

That was all the encouragement he needed. Jesse pushed my thighs together and back until my knees touched my chest. Our gazes met and locked as he started pounding into me. It was fast, hard, and the best I've ever had. My pussy began to gush with each thrust as I came again and again.

"I'm losing my mind!" He cried, still holding my gaze. I felt that if we didn't watch each other's eyes we would lose each other along the way. "It has never been like this before, Layla."

I nodded. "For me either." I assured him, gasping for air as he continued to pound into me.

"Oh GOD!" He stopped. Just completely stopped and I was scared something was wrong with him.

"Jesse?" I pushed up onto my elbows. He was still hard inside of me. His breathing was erratic and his eyes were almost scary they were so black. "Jesse, baby what's wrong?"

"Nothing." He whispered. Those strong hands of his grasped my hips and lifted me. He was still inside of me and I wrapped my legs around his lean waist so I wouldn't lose our connection. "It just felt wrong to be fucking you when what I need to do is make love to you." He held onto me tight as he thrust up into me.

It was earth shattering how fast he had went from fucking my brains out, to slow and easy love making. The night was full of firsts, because I had never made love like this before. With Jesse still on his knees and me wrapped around him. It showed me just how strong he was, the way he was taking my weight and his own while he slid in and out of me like this. But it was no less mind-blowing the way he was making me come apart for him.

I buried my face in his neck. Softly crying as he pushed me over into another orgasm. My inner muscles clamped around him for what felt like the hundredth time but he was still rock hard. The pleasure we were having in each other's arms was not something that everyone got to experience. This was special.

It felt as if our souls were coming together with each tender thrust.

It was scary as hell!

But it was a good scary. Like being on the top of a rollercoaster just as it went over into that big plunge: your stomach full of nervous anxiety, your adrenaline pumping and your heart almost carefree.

"Layla." He whispered, his breath coming in short little pants. "Layla look at me." Jesse commanded.

I raised my head. My hair was all over the place, tangled in my face, sticking to his damp chest. I tossed it out of my face so I could see him better. Sweat poured from his face, glistening on his smooth head. "Jess…"

"Tell me," he commanded.

I looked away, knowing instinctively what he wanted me to say but I couldn't. I wouldn't. Emotion clogged my throat. It wasn't possible to feel that deeply this soon. It was crazy to even think it could happen! Not with a rocker! Not with a rocker!

Not with a rocker!

"Please, Layla," he whispered. "I need to hear you say it. I want those words to be on your sweet lips when I come."

"I can't." I shook my head. "This is crazy."

"I know, baby. I know. It's crazy and scary, but it's also the best thing I've ever felt. I don't know if it's just because of how amazing we are together in bed, but I don't care. I feel the same way. Please, say the words!"

He hadn't increased his speed, but I could feel my inner muscles quickening once more. My nipples grazed across his chest with each upward thrust pushing me higher. "Jess…" I licked my lips, a sure sign that I was close. "Oh God!"

"Say it," he pleaded, a vein sticking out in his neck. He was barely hanging on.

"If I say it will you fuck me hard?" I cried.

"No. Not this time." His fingers dug into my hips, fighting his release, but he didn't stop moving inside of me.

THE ROCKER THAT SAVORS ME

"I..." I couldn't hold back any longer. I felt my desire bursting forward, my cum pooling and dripping down his dick, over his balls. I tossed my head back and cried out. "I love you!"

"Love you too," he gritted out as he emptied inside of me.

Chapter 12
Jesse

We fell onto the bed, both of us out of breath and panting hard. The complete contentment I felt at her words, followed by the most incredible orgasm I have ever experienced, left me feeling carefree. I could have floated I felt so good just then.

Layla lay under me, her breathing just as rapid as my own. We were covered in sweat, and cum, but I didn't care. I wanted to bask in this feeling for as long as possible, but I was heavy so I rolled to my side, taking her with me. One leg wrapped around both of hers, her head tucked under my chin, and my semi-hard dick still inside of her tight little pussy, I could have happily died then and there.

We lay like that for a long while. I felt her breathing even out but knew she hadn't fallen asleep. It was enough just to hold each other for now, and I didn't want to sleep through a second of it any more than she did.

"Tell me something no one else knows," she whispered sometime later.

I kissed the top of her head. "I don't think there's anything about me that Em doesn't know."

She pulled back, her brow raised at my confession. "Really?"

I shrugged. "She knows us all inside and out. She knows all my secrets just as she knows all of Drake's, Shane's, and Nik's." My fingers lazily trailed up and down her bare back. "That probably sounds nuts…"

Layla shook her head. "No. That sounds… It must be nice to have someone that you trust that much with every little secret, every dirty deed. I envy you."

I pulled back, propping my head up on my hand so I could look down at the woman who had snuck into my heart way too quickly. I knew nothing about her, but I was determined to rectify that before the end of the night. "You don't have someone you can confide in?" She shook her head. "Not even Lana?"

She grimaced. "Lana is the last person I would confide all my dark deeds to. I want her to be untouched by all the things that I've done in the past."

THE ROCKER THAT SAVORS ME

"Then tell them to me," I urged. "Confide in me. I won't judge you. Not after the life I've lived."

With a thoughtful frown, she turned onto her stomach, resting her chin on her crossed arms. "My life hasn't been pretty."

Unable to keep from touching her, I reached over and stroked my fingers through her long cinnamon colored hair. "I don't care about that. Tell me your secrets."

She turned her head so she was looking at me. "Okay." Her little pink tongue came out and moistened her bottom lip. I was transfixed for a moment, watching that wicked appendage disappear back into her hot mouth. "My mother tossed me out when I was sixteen," she told me. "She found her current sugar daddy in bed with me."

I didn't even blink at that, although the thought of her being thrown out by her mother at such a young age made my anger rise. "Go on."

She seemed surprised that I wasn't casting any kind of judgment or asking questions. "I didn't have anywhere to go, so I ended up in a shelter for a few weeks." Shame darkened her eyes, burned in her pretty cheeks. "I had to quit school. No one would hire me, a teenager who was a high school drop out."

"That must have been rough," I murmured, continuing to stroke her hair.

Layla nodded. "It was. At first. Until I met Zeke." A small smile lifted the corner of her sinful mouth. "It was raining and I was riding the bus to stay warm and dry. He got on just outside of Sunset and dropped down on the bench beside me…" She sighed. "He scared the hell out of me. All those tattoos and piercings." She raised her head, scratching her nose. "But he was the first person that was nice to me that day. He had a sack full of fast food, and I guess he could hear my stomach growling. I hadn't eaten in two days…" She grimaced and I had to force my fingers not to tangle in her hair. The thought of her hungry…I couldn't stand that. I had witnessed a hungry Emmie far too often when she was a kid. Layla being hungry…it hurt even worse than the memories of Emmie!

"He gave me the whole bag. It was full of burgers and fries. They were his dinner, but Zeke gave it all to me without saying a word about it."

A lump formed in my throat, and I wanted to meet this Zeke guy, shake his hand, and thank him for taking care of my Layla. "He sounds like a good guy," I managed in a croaky voice.

Her smile grew slightly bigger. "He was. I was a complete stranger to him. Could have been any type of person. But he fed me then took me home with him. He had an extra room since his roommate had moved to Boston. Even though he scared me, I still felt safer with him than going back to the shelter."

She was quiet for a minute and then blew out a long sigh. "Zeke owned a tattoo parlor and gave me a job. I answered the phones, kept the place clean. It wasn't much, but at least I had a little money coming in, and I didn't feel like I was mooching off him."

"Is that how you got the piercings and the tattoos?" I loved her tattoos: the snake that wrapped around her right leg started at her ankle and ended about half way up her thigh; the Celtic knots on each wrist; the little humming bird on her left shoulder blade; the crossed lightning bolts on the back of her neck. I really liked the little she devil on her right pubic bone, all red and sexy.

"Zeke had an apprentice. No one would let him work on them until they could see what he could do. I was his masterpiece." She gave me a little smirk that lit up her chocolate eyes. "I made him pay me, of course."

I grinned. "Of course."

"Zeke kept me out of trouble. Helped me get my GED so that I could get a better job. But I was busting my ass at two different jobs and still not able to keep my head above water." Her eyes turned stormy, troubled. "Zeke fell in love with some guy from Miami and moved away…and I found myself stripping."

That surprised me. I hadn't expected that at all, but it didn't matter to me. So what if she had been a stripper? It wasn't like she was whoring herself out. "How did that go?" I asked.

THE ROCKER THAT SAVORS ME

She shrugged. "It went really well. I was able to pay my bills and keep food in my fridge. I saved up enough and bought my Corolla. Life wasn't easy, but it was getting better."

I nodded, understanding what she meant. "When did Lana and Lucy come onto the scene?"

"Two years ago. Social services called me out of the blue and asked if I was willing to take in my two sisters since our mother had been killed in a car accident. At first I thought she had the wrong number. When I left, it was only Lana. I tried to keep in touch with her, but our mother wouldn't let me, so Lucy came as a complete surprise to me."

"It must have been hard working and taking on the girls like that."

"Not really. As soon as I knew they needed me, I told the social worker that I wanted them. But I couldn't keep them if I was stripping. One of my regulars at the club told me if I ever needed a job he would hire me...so I took him up on the offer. Stan, he owns Perfectly Clean, helped me out. I got a respectable job and the girls."

I think I might have fallen a little more in love with her as she told me about her life. Not just how she came to be the surrogate mother of her two younger sisters, but how she had come to be the person she was today. Layla had spirit, tenacity. She was full of life, even though life had tried to beat her down more than a few times. Her courage, diligence, and determination were all in her eyes, and I liked seeing them there.

She reminded me of Emmie.

It wasn't a bad thing. In fact, I think I had secretly been looking for someone like her my whole life. Someone who could deal with me without giving up on me. Someone who would love me even when I was a completely unlovable bastard. I could be a real asshole at times, especially when I thought about life before we had hit it big, or the years before we had gotten Emmie back.

We talked until the sun came up, and she fell asleep in my arms. When I finally gave into sleep, I did so with a content smile on my face...

The buzzing of a phone woke me. Groaning, I untangled myself from Layla and searched for my jeans. By the time I found them, the phone had stopped ringing, but I knew that if it was Emmie it would start ringing again soon. I pulled my phone from my pocket and saw that it was after two in the afternoon. Muttering a curse, I saw that I had six missed calls, all of them from Emmie in the last hour.

Worry for her made my fingers shake as I hit redial on the last number and waited for her to pick up. "Are you okay?" she demanded as soon as she answered.

"I was going to ask you the same thing," I told her, running a hand over the small stubble on my head.

She sighed. "I'm fine. I was just worried about you. Lana came over asking if I had heard from you or Layla. She's worried about her sister and can't get her to answer her phone. Where are you, Jesse?"

"We crashed at Tom's," I told her and heard her sigh again. "It isn't like that."

"Sure it isn't. Shane *never* takes his one-nighters there." She sounded disappointed in me and I hated that. "Tell Layla to call her sister."

"Em!" I pressed the phone closer to my ear. "I swear to you that this isn't like that. Layla means more to me than that."

She was quiet for a full minute before she spoke again. "Okay. We can talk later. Love you." Before I could tell her I loved her too, she hung up.

Muttering under my breath, I tossed the phone aside and started gathering the rest of my clothes. Layla was still out cold on the bed. I didn't want to disturb her, so I moved as quietly as I could to the connecting bathroom and shut the door. I needed a shower. I smelled of sweat and sex. Not that those were terrible smells, but I didn't want to go home with Layla's juices all over me. I didn't want the guys to know what she smelled like. It was a crazy thing to worry about, but true nonetheless.

Layla

THE ROCKER THAT SAVORS ME

The smell of strong brewed coffee woke me. I moaned, turning over onto my back. Slowly, I cracked open one eye first and then the other. Jesse, sexy as hell in only a pair of boxers, stood over me with two mugs in hand. One brow was raised and he was grinning down at me. My heart melted even more and I heard the words that he had forced me to say last night echo in my mind.

"What time is it?" I muttered as I sat up, not caring that I was naked and the covers had slipped to my waist. I liked the way his eyes rapidly switched from a soft brown to onyx in a split second.

"Three."

I muttered a curse and jumped out of bed. Three in the afternoon! I hadn't even called Lana to let her know I wasn't coming home. Fuck, talk about irresponsible. How was I to expect my seventeen year old sister to act responsibly if I wasn't doing the same thing? I found my jeans and dug my phone out of the back hip pocket.

Sure enough I had six missed calls and my text box was overflowing.

"Calm down." Jesse told me. "I already talked to Emmie. The girls are fine, just worried about you. Give Lana a text to tell her you will be home in a little while."

I grimaced. "I haven't been much of a good influence."

"No one is perfect. And it's not like you left them all alone. Lana is old enough to take care of Lucy for one night. And if they needed anything Em and the guys were right next door." He offered me a mug of coffee and I took it with a grateful smile.

"I know that. But…" I took a sip of the coffee and nearly choked on whatever was in the cup. It tasted like coffee—strong coffee—but it was so thick I thought I was eating it instead of drinking the stuff. "What is this?" I got out in a croaky voice.

"Jesse's special cup of Joe." He informed me with a sly grin. "It puts hair on the chest. The guys live by it…Em, not so much. Do you like it?"

Was it bad that I already felt twitchy from the caffeine? Oh, fuck I was going to be up for days on this stuff. "Does it have speed in it?"

Jesse sighed. "Okay, so maybe I use more coffee than water. But when you live on the road you learn to survive off this stuff." He took a big swallow from his own mug. "Are you hungry? We can stop for a bite on the way home. Or pick up something."

I gave him back the coffee. "Or I could cook when we get back." I picked up my clothes spread around the room and headed for the bathroom. "Give me five minutes." I needed a shower, but I would have to make do with a quick rinse under the spray.

"Layla…" At the door I stopped when I heard Jesse's voice. Turning I found him where I had left him, looking…His entire body looked like it was made of stone as he stood there watching me. His erection sticking out from his body. His arms tense with desire. His obvious need for me made me melt all over again.

I swallowed hard, and with trembling fingers I got out a quick text to Lana before my mind went blank. I think it said I wouldn't be home until later, but I couldn't be sure. Because as soon as I hit send I tossed it and my clothes back on the floor and ran across the room. He had already gotten rid of the coffee mugs because his arms caught me against him and lifted me in the air.

"I need to be inside of you so fucking bad, baby." He breathed against my lips as he slowly lowered me. My body pressed against every inch of his as he carefully sat me on my feet. "Are you on the pill?"

"No." I told him, not worried about birth control as I licked my way across his chest from one nipple to the other.

"Fuck!" He roared and tossed me on the bed. "I only had one condom."

My body was already screaming for him. Trying to clear the desire fog from my brain I started doing math in my head. Swallowing hard I nodded. "I have never had sex without a condom before." I told him honestly.

"Me either." He ran his hands over his head in a way that told me he was frustrated. "And I'm clean, Layla. Em makes us all get tested every six months or so. I just had a complete checkup three months ago…"

THE ROCKER THAT SAVORS ME

I breathed a sigh of relief. "I'm clean too." I assured him. "I haven't even had sex in like three years. I had a physical when I started working for Perfectly Clean."

His eyes darkened. His body seeming to actually grow bigger as he crawled toward me on the bed. "Are you willing to chance it?" He demanded in an almost animalistic sounding voice.

I licked my lips nervously. "It isn't much of a risk. Right now is a safe time in my cycle. Trust me on this. I'm the most regular person you will ever meet. I could tell you down to the hour when I will get my period."

"Oh fuck." He breathed, stopping between my spread thighs and setting back on his heels. "Layla..."

He didn't have to say anything more. I knew exactly what was going through his head, because it was going through mine too. Last night had been amazing. I had lost a part of myself to him last night, not just my heart. And to make love without anything separating us! That might just kill us. "Come inside me, Jesse." I pleaded, trailing my fingers across his stomach. "I'm ready for you."

"I'll try to keep my head." He promised as he gently pushed my thighs further apart. I watched in total fascination as he rubbed his bare dick across my outer lips. When that pink, mushroom shaped head slipped across my clit I cried out in pleasure so intense it arched my back.

Jesse gritted his teeth as he held his dick in his hand and rubbed it back and f across my hardened clit, making my already wet pussy flood with liquid desire. I gripped his forearms, my nails sinking into his skin as my head thrashed almost incoherently. "So wet. So slick. Your pussy is beautiful, baby."

"Put it inside me. NOW!" I cried out in desperation.

Sweat was already beading on his forehead and upper lip. Drops dripped onto his chest and my stomach. I moaned at the sweet torture of it. Still, he played with me, rubbing that beautiful cock of his back and forth, up and down, in little circles. I was hanging on to the edge of a mind numbing orgasm by my fingertips.

THE ROCKER THAT SAVORS ME

Moaning, I released my hold on his forearms and pinched my nipples. I tugged on them hard, so hard that I lifted each breast towards him. Jolts of pleasure went straight to my pussy and I began to pant. "Ah...Ah...Oh!" I cried. "Oh! Oh! Oh!" I thrust my hips up, trying to force him to slip lower. I could smell the muskiness of his pre-cum already, knew that he was just as lost as I was, and we hadn't even started.

"Oh, God!" Tears slipped from my eyes it felt so good. "Jesse, please," I sobbed. "I need you now."

With an animal like growl, he thrust in me so deep and hard I thought he bruised the walls of my uterus. But it was so good! So amazingly good that it sent me over the edge. My inner muscles contracted hard, and I watched in amazement as his eyes rolled back in his head. He didn't move after that first hard thrust, but he didn't have to. My orgasm was milking his own from him. His mouth opened in a silent scream. It was so sexy, so hot that it intensified my own release.

He seemed frozen like that for nearly a full minute before his muscles started to relax. We were both breathing hard, sweat pouring off of us both. Jesse groaned and fell on top of me, crushing my breasts between us, but I didn't care. I loved the feel of him against me like this. Still hard inside of me while the mixture of our release soaked the sheets under me, he held me tight.

My hands went around him, and I skimmed my fingers up and down his back. Goose flesh popped up along the trail, and I turned my head to lick his neck. He tasted both sweet and salty. His scent invaded my every sense, and I begged God to give me just a few more minutes of this paradise.

Chapter 13
Layla

By the time we got back to Malibu it was late.

Jesse pulled up into the driveway in front of the beach house and reluctantly turned off the Escalade's engine. I bit my lip, not wanting to part with him any more than he wanted to from me. We had made love so many times I had lost count. That room back in his friend's house had reeked of sex when we left, but I hadn't even cared.

Gently, fingers grasped and intertwined with mine. With a sad sigh, he brought our joined hands to his lips and kissed each finger. "Is it selfish that I want to keep you to myself for another night?"

I leaned my head back against the seat and smiled up at him. "No. Not selfish at all because I want the same thing. Too bad that we can't have everything that we want…"

"Fuck that," he muttered heatedly. "I'll fix it so that we can have every night together, Layla."

I frowned. "How are you going to do that?" I asked.

"What does that mean?"

He was already shaking his head. "Don't worry about it." Leaning in, he kissed me, making me forget anything he had just said. His fingers tangled in my already horribly knotted hair and pulled me closer. I wanted to climb across the console and straddle him, have sex with him right here in the driveway!

He pulled back just enough to press his forehead against mine. "Go, Layla," he whispered. "Go before I do something crazy like drive back to Beverly Hills."

"Jesse…"

"Please, go. I'm not strong enough to…" He released me and fell back against his seat, his eyes closed tight. "Good night, baby. I'll call you in the morning."

When he didn't move to open his door, I slowly reached for my own. "Good night, Jesse," I whispered before slipping from the SUV.

Swallowing hard to keep my tears from spilling out and making me sob, I walked quickly back to the guesthouse. How

THE ROCKER THAT SAVORS ME

crazy was it that I didn't want to be away from him for even a night? My heart was actually aching, clenching more and more with each step that took me away from him.

No, no, no! No! Last night—when I had told him I loved him—that had just been in the heat of the moment. It wasn't true. It wasn't. I couldn't be in love with him this soon, this deeply!

But my heart was saying that I was a liar…

Muttering curses under my breath, I opened the door to the guesthouse and walked inside. Lucy was watching television in the living room with a plate of Chinese food in front of her. I stopped and dropped a kiss on her dark head. "Hey, baby doll. Where's Lana?"

"In the shower," Lucy informed me around a mouthful of fried rice and shrimp. "We went swimming with Drake earlier, and she was itching."

I smiled. "So she and Drake made up?"

Lucy nodded, her attention going back to the television and the episode of Sponge Bob that was on. "Yep. We spent the whole afternoon with him. Then he ordered Chinese, which is awesome, but he left when I had to take my bath."

"Well, I'm glad you two had a good time." I placed another kiss on her sweet smelling head and turned towards the bedroom. "It's getting late, sweetheart. As soon as Sponge Bob goes off head to bed, okay?"

"Okay," she called after me.

The shower was still running when I walked into the bathroom. I could hear Lana humming happily over the running water and couldn't help smiling to myself. "Hey!" I called to her as I sat on the edge of the toilet seat.

The shower curtain pulled back enough, and Lana's head peeked around. She gave me a sly grin. "Hello, stranger. Enjoy your date? A date that lasted more than twenty-four freaking hours?"

I was sure that I was glowing with just how much I had enjoyed myself. "It was the most amazing night of my life." That was as much detail as my seventeen year old sister was getting. "I heard you had some company this afternoon. So you and Drake are okay now?"

"More than okay." She pulled the shower curtain back but didn't stop talking as she continued to shower. "He apologized to me, I forgave him, and then we went swimming. After that, he came over here and we watched movies and ordered dinner. I didn't want him to go back to the main house, but it was getting late and Lucy needed a bath."

"Sounds like you guys enjoyed yourselves."

"I enjoy every minute with Drake…no matter what we are doing," Lana muttered more to herself than to me.

I sighed. "Lana…"

The water turned off and the curtain snapped back. "Stop worrying so much about it, Layla. I'm not stupid. I know that he's thirteen years older than me. I know that I don't stand a chance with him. We are just friends. I know. I know. I know!" She jerked a towel off the hanger and wrapped it around herself almost angrily, but when she stepped from the tub and faced me she was smiling, even if it didn't quiet reach her eyes. "Just. Friends."

I stood and pulled her into my arms. "Okay." I kissed her check, pretending like I believed her. While it might be true for Drake that they were just friends, I knew my sister, and what she was feeling was far stronger than mere friendship. I could see the truth in her eyes.

Lana was in love with Drake.

Jesse

I wanted to talk to Emmie as soon as I got home. I had things that I needed her to handle for me. Nik said that she was asleep, and I didn't want to bother her if she was comfortable. She had been having insomnia lately, and if she was finally getting some sleep, I wasn't about to interrupt that.

So I put all the things I needed to do to the back of my mind for now and dropped down on the sectional with my band brothers. It was just the four of us doing nothing more than watching football and drinking beer. It felt good to relax with them.

Half time came and Shane got up to get us all more beers. Drake was tossing back Jack Daniels and chasing it with his beer. It was the first time I had actually seen him with a bottle in a week, and I had already gotten use to him being sober. I watched as he swallowed glass after glass and hated that I was witnessing the old Drake, not the new one that had laughed more in the past week than I had ever heard from him in the lifetime that I had known him.

When the bottle was empty, I took it from his slackened fingers and pulled him up. "Let's go, Drake," I urged softly. "Time for bed."

He sighed but didn't resist. He stumbled a little as I helped him up the stairs. In his room, he just fell onto the bed, and I took off his shoes and jeans. I wasn't going to let him just pass out, not without an explanation. "So, what happened? You and Lana have a fight?"

"Yesterday," he confirmed. "Crazy girl didn't want me buying her things. Said that I was trying to buy her." Drake laughed but it in no way held humor. "But I apologized today."

"She didn't forgive you?"

"Nope. She did. Spent the rest of the day with her and Lucy." His words were getting a little slurred now, but I had years of experience learning how to understand drunk Drake. "One of the best days of my life," he muttered so low that I almost didn't hear him.

I frowned. "So why the fuck are you drinking?"

Drake's eyes were about to close when they snapped open and he glared up at me. "Because I want her so fucking much! Because I feel like I need her to breathe. Because she's seventeen fucking years old!" he shouted at me.

I dropped down on the edge of his bed, facing my friend who was so troubled with himself. "Dray, she's beautiful. A blind man could see how beautiful she is. And it isn't just on the outside. She's really sweet, man. Lana is special."

A tear leaked from the corner of his eye. "I know that," he whispered.

"And I think she has some strong feelings for you too." The few times I had actually seen them together I had witnessed the way Lana looked at Drake. I had worried about her feeling too much for my friend. That she would get in over her head with an infatuation that she would quickly outgrow. But after talking to Layla until the sun came up that morning, I also knew that the girl was more mature than most thirty-year-olds I knew. She was wise for her years.

But to Drake her age was a major problem. There was a reason why he always ended up with the cougars that followed us from city to city on our tours. He never looked twice at the younger girls that tried to get into our beds. He was scared to death of being labeled a pedophile. "What are you going to do?" I asked after we had both been quiet for a few minutes.

Drake scrubbed a hand across his damp eyes. "Nothing."

I bit back a curse. "Nothing? So you just go on being friends but kill yourself with alcohol to numb your pain?"

He shrugged. "I can't touch her. I *won't* touch her!"

Frustrated, I ran a hand over my head, hating the stubble that I felt under my fingers. "Have you at least talked to her about this?"

"No. She's too young to understand. I'm not going to burden her with it all." He closed his eyes, already drifting off to sleep. "Thanks for taking care of me, man," he muttered as he passed out.

I glared down at my friend. He looked at peace in sleep now, but soon the nightmares would invade that peace and I would hear his screams from my room. I was sure that the alcohol made the dreams that much worse, but there was no explaining that to Drake. Muttering curses under my breath, I tugged the comforter up around him and left the room.

There was nothing more I could do tonight, perhaps nothing more I could ever do. Drake refused to talk about his nightmares with any of us, especially Shane, and I wasn't going to tell his secrets to Lana. If she was to ever truly understand him, then she would have to know all of it, but I wasn't going to be that person.

Instead of going back downstairs, I went down the hall and fell onto my own bed. It was late, so I couldn't call Layla. I ached to have her lying beside of me, and not just to soothe the ache in my dick. Thinking about Drake and his nightmares had put my cock into hiding, but I still ached to hold her, talk to her about all of this.

Would she understand and know what to do? Should I confide in her? I was at a loss. If I told her, she could possibly turn away, even refuse to let Lana see Drake again. That would only hurt Drake more, not to mention break a confidence I had made almost fifteen years ago. But if I didn't tell her…

"Ah, fuck," I grunted. "I'm screwed either way."

Somehow, I fell asleep only to jerk awake around two thirty. Drake was having it rougher than usual tonight while he fought with the demons from his past and his own conscience regarding Lana. I sat up in bed, my fist clenched in the covers beside of me, while I listened to him sobbing. I was just about to go wake him up when I heard Emmie.

I jumped out of bed, not bothering to put on pants over my boxers. I walked down the hall to Drake's open door. Emmie was lying beside of him with his face buried in her neck while she rubbed his back. "It's okay, Drake," she whispered softly. "You're safe. Shh. Shh. You're safe."

I stood there until Drake had slipped back into a restless sleep while Emmie continued to soothe him. After a while, she drifted off to sleep too, and I moved into the room to cover them both up. Turning, I was surprised to see Shane standing in the doorway. He was covered in sweat, telling me that he had been out for a run. I grimaced.

The brothers handled their disturbed past differently: Drake with his alcohol and Shane with sex. When he couldn't get that readily, he'd run until he couldn't feel his legs. I met my friend's blue gray eyes, and Shane quickly looked away. "Maybe we should make him see a specialist again."

"That didn't work out so well last time. Or the two times we talked him into rehab," I reminded him quietly. Drake had lasted a week the first time in rehab. The second time he had put a male nurse through a window and they had kicked him out. The psychologist hadn't fared much better. He had gone too far too soon, and Drake hadn't been ready for that. For a month afterward,

Emmie had slept almost every night with him because the nightmares had been too much.

"He seemed like he was getting better," Shane whispered, looking over at his sleeping older brother. "I thought Lana was helping."

"She was. She is." I grimaced. "But he's also fighting himself and his feelings for her. Maybe when she's older…"

"Yeah, maybe." Shane turned to go. "If he lives that long."

…Emmie…

I was startled awake by the feel of strong arms lifting me. Blinking open my eyes, I looked up at Nik who was holding me against his warm, bare chest. In the background, I vaguely heard gagging and realized it was Drake throwing up and remembered I had spent part of the night in bed with him.

Warm lips brushed across my forehead, and I leaned into his kiss. "What time is it?"

"Still pretty early," Nik murmured softly as he carried me down the hall to our room. The door was already open, and he kicked it shut behind him before putting me in the middle of the bed.

I glanced at the clock to see that it was barely after six and grimaced. Any hopes of snuggling in bed with Nik for a little while were lost. Sighing, I arranged myself so I was lying on my side and wrapped my legs around the body pillow so my hips wouldn't ache as bad. The baby was getting bigger by the day, and my hips seemed to do nothing but hurt.

To my surprise, Nik crawled in behind me and pulled my back against his chest. My heart filled with love, and I fought the urge to cry happy tears. "Don't you have to be at the studio soon?"

He kissed my neck making me shiver. My nipples instantly hardened, but we both knew that there wasn't going to be any action. I hated it, but it hurt to make love lately. Nik understood and never complained about it. "Not going in until later. Screw them. I want to hold you for a little while."

THE ROCKER THAT SAVORS ME

One big hand skimmed over my stomach, played with the protruding belly button that had popped out about a month ago, and then settled low where our baby liked to punch me. That little girl was silent this morning, but all too soon she would be using me as her personal punching bag.

Tired, content to be in my love's arms, I pushed all the things that were on my mind to the back and let sleep take me…

Sometime later, I felt Nik leave me. He brushed a tender kiss across my cheek then another across my exposed stomach. I sighed happily and buried my face in my pillow. "Love you, baby," he whispered.

"Love you."

I fell back into a dreamless sleep and didn't wake up again until midmorning. I hadn't been sleeping well lately. Restless legs, aching hips, and just an all-around uncomfortable feeling had made me an insomniac. Last night was the first good sleep I had in what felt like forever, but I was still feeling exhausted when I climbed out of bed and tossed on a pair of yoga pants and one of Nik's old shirts.

I couldn't care less how I looked. My hair was a mess, and I didn't even bother to brush it as I pulled it into a sloppy bun. My feet were swollen, and it hurt to walk down the stairs, but I had things to do that couldn't wait.

From the kitchen, I could smell bacon frying, but for once the smell didn't make my mouth water. In fact, I felt sick and had to hold my breath as I passed the kitchen on my way to my office. "I'm not hungry, Layla," I called to her.

I heard her moving around, and a few moments later she appeared in my office doorway. She wore a concerned expression as she looked me over. "You look green, Emmie. Call your doctor."

A small smile teased my lips, and I was ever thankful that whatever god had sent this woman to me had. In just a few weeks, I had developed a bond with Layla. For the first time in my life, I had a female friend, and I actually liked it. "I will, but first I have to take care of a few things."

Layla raised a brow. Crossing her arms over her generous chest, she leaned against the door jamb of my office and looked as if she wasn't going to budge anytime soon. "I think you should call now."

I sighed and picked up my cellphone. After scrolling through my contacts, I pressed connect and waited for Dr. Chesterfield's nurse to answer. When she did, I told her I wasn't feeling well and the woman asked me to come in. Sighing, I took a quick peek at the clock. It was after eleven. There was so much to do and all the guys were at the studio.

Biting my lips, I glanced at Layla. "Can you drive me to my doctor? They want me to come in, but I can't drive." My stomach had gotten so big that I couldn't steer a vehicle without hurting myself.

Layla smiled. "Sure."

I stood with difficulty and grabbed the keys to Shane's car, along with my purse and phone. Really, I was going to have to make Nik buy another SUV. Shane's car was pretty to look at and a dream to drive, but not all that safe to be in. Crazy how I worried about car safety now when it had never even crossed my mind before I had found out I was pregnant.

Thirty minutes later, I was being poked and prodded by the misogynist doctor that was supposed to be the best in all of California. Alexis Moreitti had recommended him to me. I trusted her judgment when it came to who was taking care of her baby, so I had started seeing him too, but when he had his fingers inside of me, moving them around like he was now, I really hated the prick. Layla gave my hand a little squeeze in support, and I squeezed back, thankful to have her there with me. After a moment, the doctor stepped back and pulled off his gloves. Turning, he began washing his hands. "You are dilated to a two," he informed me.

I raised a brow. "What does that mean?" I knew that when a woman was dilated to a ten it was time to push the baby out. "Isn't it too soon to be dilating?" It was wasn't even the middle of September. I still had seven weeks to go before my baby was due.

Dr. Chesterfield gave me a reassuring smile. "Some women can go months dilated at two or even three. This is perfectly normal. All the discomfort you are feeling is normal. Your nausea isn't so much, but I can give you something which won't hurt the baby to ease that." He pulled a prescription pad from his coat pocket and started scribbling. "Take it easy for a few days, Emmie. Stay off your feet as much as possible and don't put yourself in any stressful situations. I want to see you again next week. Bring Nik too because we need to set a date to do your C-section."

"Great," I muttered, taking the prescription from him.

Layla gave my shoulder a little squeeze, and I put my hand over hers. The doctor gave her a meaningful look. "Make sure she takes it easy. Have those guys of hers tie her to the bed for a few days if you have to."

Layla nodded. "Of course," she assured him. "I'll do it myself if I have to."

THE ROCKER THAT SAVORS ME

Chapter 14
Layla

When we got home, I was quick to get Emmie up to her room. She didn't protest much, probably because along with the prescription, they had also given her a shot as a precaution. The shot, some kind of strong anti-nausea medication, was making her sleepy. The doctor didn't want to chance Emmie getting dehydrated should she start throwing up.

As soon as I got her to her room, I helped her change into pajamas. I tucked her into bed like a child. She rested her head back on her pillow and pulled her body pillow closer. "I think I owe you a bonus, Layla. Your job description doesn't cover taking care of the sick pregnant woman."

Her words upset me, and I had to blink back a few tears. "If you even dare to pay me for this, I will shove the check down your pretty little throat," I told her.

Emmie blinked up at me, surprised at my quivering voice. "Layla…"

"You pay me to clean this house. I'm taking care of you because you're my friend and I care about you. Don't you ever say anything like that again."

Her hand grasped mine, and I noticed that her fingers were ice cold. "Layla, I'm sorry. It was a joke." Tears filled her eyes and spilled over. "Thank you for taking care of me today. No one, other than the guys, has ever cared enough to take care of me—to be there holding my hand the way that you have today."

I wiped my free hand across my eyes. "You are my friend, Emmie. Of course I'm going to take care of you when you need it." I dropped a kiss on her forehead like I would if I was talking to Lana or Lucy. In such a short span of time, Emmie had become another sister to me. "Are you hungry?" I asked gently.

She gave me a weak smile. "Not really, but I guess I should try something. The baby hasn't moved around a whole lot, and I think she needs something to wake her up."

"Okay. Just relax. I'll get you something that won't be harsh on your stomach." I gave her hand a squeeze then tucked it under the covers with the rest of her to get warm.

In the kitchen, I fixed a can of chicken soup and some dry toast. A glass of fizzy lemon-lime soda and a dish of some melon sorbet rounded out the little meal I had put together on a tray for Emmie. Before I could pick up the tray, my cell rang and I fished it out of my back pocket. Without glancing at the caller ID, I hit connect and put it to my ear. "This is Layla."

"How has your day been?"

Jesse's sexy as sin voice in my ear made me shiver. I stopped what I was doing and leaned against the counter. "It's been an adventure," I assured him then told him about taking Emmie to the doctor and what the man had said. The more I said, the more I could feel his tension through the phone.

There was a pause, then he blew out a pent up breath. "How is she feeling now?"

I could hear his frustration and his love for her. It warmed me from the inside out that a big, bad rock star could feel so deeply for someone other than himself. It went against everything I had ever seen before in other rockers, namely my own father. Maybe it was okay to love this guy after all. "I'm making her something to eat. She's a little out of it after the shot of anti-nausea medication that Dr. Chesterfield gave her."

"Thank you for taking care of her, Layla. That…It means a lot to me, baby."

I wrapped my free arm around myself, trying to hold the feelings I had for this man inside. "Don't thank me," I whispered. "Emmie is my friend, too. Friends take care of each other."

"Yes they do," he murmured in a thoughtful tone.

"When will you be home?" I questioned, excited to see him.

"Probably as soon as I tell Nik about Emmie. Want to have dinner with me, tonight? I know a kid friendly place that we could take Lucy. I'm sure she would love their mac and cheese. Crap, I order it every time I go."

My heart literally skipped a beat. I had to swallow a few times to get the emotional lump from my throat. He was including Lucy.

THE ROCKER THAT SAVORS ME

It didn't all together surprise me, not after seeing him with her and seeing how good he was with kids, but considering he had asked me out and thought of her too...? Oh, fuck. Yes, it was true. I loved this rocker. "That sounds like fun," I stuttered.

"It's a date then." He paused as if he wanted to say something more. Instead, he just murmured, "Bye, sweetheart."

I stood there with the phone pressed to my ear for almost a full minute before I snapped out of my daze. I was in love with Jesse Thornton. Crazy, obsessive love. The kind that would make me stupid and heartsick, but I really didn't care anymore. I wanted this. My heart needed this.

With a dopey smile on my face, I lifted the tray and carried it up to Emmie's room. She was just barely dozing and opened her eyes when I walked in. She tried to sit up, and I hurried to set the tray down on the bedside table so I could help her get comfortable. I fluffed pillows and arranged them behind her then put the tray across her lap.

I sat with her while she sipped the broth from the chicken soup and nibbled on the toast. She devoured the sorbet and even asked for more when her bowl was empty. When I returned with her second serving, she looked better. She was sitting back against the pillows rubbing her hand lovingly over her stomach, murmuring to it. "She's kicking up a storm again," Emmie told me with a happy smile that made her light up from the inside out.

"Good." I sat the dish on her tray.

I stayed with her until I heard the Escalade pull into the driveway outside. I had the tray in my hands when the front door slammed shut and footsteps came running up the stairs. Seconds later, Nik appeared in the doorway, his face pale and his unique blue eyes looking wild. "Em?" he croaked out.

"I'm fine, Nik." She rushed to assure him. "Layla has taken great care of me."

I gave him a small smile as I moved by him, but he grabbed my elbow, stopping me. I looked up in curiosity because I felt his fingers trembling. He blinked a few times then looked down at me. "Thank you, Layla," he whispered.

THE ROCKER THAT SAVORS ME

It bothered me that they all found it hard to believe that someone had taken time to make sure that Emmie was taken care of, that anyone other than the five of them would want to take care of them. I found myself repeating the same thing I had been saying all afternoon. "Don't thank me. She's my friend."

I didn't think he heard me because he was already moving towards the bed, so I closed the door behind me and took the tray down to the kitchen. The refrigerator door was open and Jesse stood there pulling out a beer. Without questioning myself, I set the tray on the counter and then moved up behind him so I could wrap my arms around his waist from behind. "Hey," I murmured, kissing his left shoulder blade.

Jesse turned and pulled me against his chest. I didn't hesitate when he lowered his head and started kissing me. My lips welcomed his, letting him in to taste me just as I wanted to taste him. The hand not holding the beer gripped my ass and pulled me even closer, right up against the ever growing evidence of his need for me. I moaned, loving how much I could affect him with just a kiss.

When we pulled apart, neither of us could catch our breaths. "What time does Lucy get home from school?" he demanded, his voice sounding rough.

I glanced at the watch on my wrist. "Her bus gets here in about thirty minutes."

His eyes darkened, and I had learned that it was a sure sign that he was about to devour me. "That's plenty of time," he growled. His beer disappeared and then I was in his arms, my legs wrapped tightly around his waist.

For such a big man, he moved quickly. Before I could even guess where he was taking me, we were in the laundry room. He sat me on the edge of the washer and started tugging on the hem of my shirt. My own fingers were busy working on his fly, anxious to get his big, beautiful cock free so I could look, touch, and taste him.

My bra went flying, and then he jerked my pants down. I lifted my hips enough to help him, and then he was on his knees. I bit my lip to keep from screaming when his tongue plunged inside of me.

My fingers gripped his smooth head and held him close while he ate me until I was on the very edge.

Trembling, I pushed his head away. "You, Jesse. I need you!"

He licked my arousal from his lips, some actually dripping from his chin, a testament to how much I needed him. "Is it still safe?"

I knew what he was asking, was it still safe for him to go bare. I didn't even think about it. Nodding, I reached for his silk covered, steel erection and positioned him at my opening. "Fuck me." I breathed in desperate need.

He stilled just as the head of his dick slipped inside. "This is not fucking," he whispered. "Tell me you understand that."

"Yes."

"Say it," he commanded, sliding another inch inside of me in slow torture.

I licked my lips. "This isn't fucking."

Another inch. "What is it then, Layla?"

I was caught in those mesmerizing eyes of his as they swirled with need and darkened with an emotion I was just coming to accept. "Making love," I whispered.

"Why is it making love?" he demanded in a voice filled with so many different things that it made my head swim trying to figure them all out.

"Because I love you," I assured him, and this time it didn't terrify the hell out me when I admitted it.

"Say it again."

"I love you, Jesse." He slammed all the way inside of me, making me cry out in pleasure.

Fingers tangled in my hair, pulling my head back enough so he was looking into them. It felt as if he could see to my very soul. "I love you, Layla." His words were like a promise, one that I hoped he would never break.

Jesse

Making love to Layla was a do or die kind of thing. If I didn't make love to her, I felt like was going to die. Sure, it was a fast and hard loving, but it was in no way a causal fuck in the laundry room. It would never be causal with me and Layla. It would never be fucking.

I thrust into her again, whispering that I loved her against the shell of her ear. She answered me with a muffled cry against my chest, her nails bit into my back with a delicious pain filled pleasure. I wanted to take it slow, but time was against us, and I pumped in and out of her at piston speed. Her moans filled the room, my heavy breathing loud in my ears.

With each thrust I felt the inner walls of her pussy clamp down harder. I felt my balls tightening, telling me that I was close. It felt so good to be bare inside of her that I couldn't control myself. I wanted to fill her with my come, the thought alone making me ready to burst.

"Jesse!" she screamed my name, and I covered her mouth with my own to drown out her cries. I felt her pussy flood with her cum, quickly followed by her inner walls convulsing with spasm after spasm. Each one milked me of my own release, and I bit down on her lip to keep my shout inside.

For a few minutes, I just stood there holding her, kissing away the hurt I had caused by biting her. I tasted her blood on my tongue and raised my head to inspect the damage I had caused. There was a tiny cut on her bottom lip, a drop of blood beading on it. I licked it away, distraught that I had hurt her like this. "I'm sorry."

She grinned. "Don't be. I liked it." She sucked the lip into her mouth. "That was amazing."

"Yes it was," I agreed and reluctantly stepped back. There was a stack of towels on the folding table behind me, and I took one to wipe her clean of our combined fluids before doing the same to myself. When we were clean, I tucked my dick back into my boxers and jeans and helped her put her bra back on.

"Do you think anyone heard us?" she asked when she was dressed.

I shook my head. "Nik will still be with Em. Drake and Shane didn't come home with us." Drake had gotten a text from Lana before I had even called Layla. She was having car trouble, and he and Shane had gone to help her. I hoped that the thing wasn't fixable. Maybe then Drake could talk Lana into letting him buy her a new car and I could get Layla her own. I hated for either of them to drive that old Corolla.

Layla combed her fingers through her tangled hair. "I need to get Lucy off the bus. Are we still on for dinner?"

"Definitely." I pulled her close for a quick kiss, loving the way she sighed and leaned into me. "I need to grab a shower and then we can go."

"Me too."

"I'll come over in about an hour then," I promised her and let her go when she pulled away. Before she could open the door, I stopped her. "Layla?" I needed her to understand something. It was important that she knew. When she turned back with a question in her chocolate brown eyes, I told her the truth. "I love you, Layla."

I saw something like relief flash across her face, and I knew that I had guessed right. The two times I had told her I loved her had been in the heat of the moment with me buried deep inside her. She probably thought that I said that to every girl I had sex with. "I've only ever said that to one other woman, baby," I informed her. "And she's upstairs with one of my best friend."

"I love you too, Jesse," she told me. "I've never said that to another guy, ever." With a smile, she opened the door and walked away, leaving me standing there with the feeling that I had been kicked in the ribs.

It took me a few minutes to get my heart under control again after her confession. I missed her already, so I rushed upstairs and jumped into the shower. I rushed the process, skipping a second shave for the day just so I could get to her sooner. I made sure that my shirt didn't have any holes and my jeans were a pair of the newer ones that Emmie had bought me. It was bad that I didn't buy things for myself, but I would have to learn to change that with what I had planned for the future.

When I was dressed, I went down the hall to check on Emmie. Layla had worried me to death when she first told me that Emmie hadn't been feeling well today. Every time she was sick, I got flashes of the time she ended up in the hospital from dehydration. She could have died if Axton hadn't been there to help her.

I knocked on the closed bedroom door then walked in. Emmie was lying on her side with Nik tucked behind her holding her close. When she saw me she smiled. "Hey."

"How are you feeling?" I asked, leaning over to kiss her cheek.

"Tired. Those meds the doctor gave me make me sleepy, but at least I don't feel like throwing up."

I rubbed a hand over her swollen stomach before dropping a kiss on it through her sleep shirt. "I'm taking Layla and Lucy out for some dinner. Want me to bring you guys back anything?"

Nik shook his head. "I'll just grab a sandwich."

"Layla already fed me." Emmie yawned. "Go, have fun."

I nodded but didn't turn for the door right away. I needed to talk to Emmie about my plans, but I wasn't sure if now was the best time. If I was really honest with myself I was scared of what her reaction was going to be. I didn't want to upset her. Not now, not ever. "Em…"

Her eyes were almost closed, but they snapped open. She must have heard something in my voice, and she reached for my hand. "It's okay. I know…" Her chin trembled but she gave me a smile. "We can talk more tomorrow."

"Love you, Em," I whispered, dropping another kiss on her cheek.

"Love you, Jesse."

THE ROCKER THAT SAVORS ME

Chapter 15
Layla

Two weeks passed in what felt like the blink of an eye. Each day was much like the same, and I always went to bed with a smile on my face. Nik and the guys didn't go into the studio the rest of the first week. He was glued to Emmie's side, making sure that she didn't get out of bed for long. By that weekend she was feeling much better without the aid of the anti-nausea medication and her feet weren't as swollen as they had been.

I liked having all the guys around during the day. I made them breakfast and lunch, did their laundry, and they kept me smiling all day long. Shane with his wicked sense of humor, Drake with his quiet sincerity, and Nik with the way he was so tender with Emmie. Then there was Jesse, who seemed to be there every time I turned around. Not that I was complaining about that.

He would sneak up behind me while I was doing dishes or cooking. Those sweet little kisses to my neck and shoulder never failed to make me wet. His whispers of "I love you" or "I need you" and even "I want you now" made me so happy I thought I was going to burst apart at the seams with it. More than once he had cornered me in the laundry room while I was working. Each time he left me spent yet still needing more.

In the evenings, he had dinner with me and Lucy. Lana sometimes joined us, and sometimes Drake joined us too. After dinner, if we were home, the three of us would walk on the beach. Lucy gathered shells and other little treasures while Jesse and I walked hand in hand behind her. After Lucy was tucked into bed, we sat on the couch watching television together. It felt like we were teenagers because we always ended up making out. When he left me each night, it was reluctantly on both our parts. I wanted to sleep in his arms, and he wanted me to be sleeping there too.

At the end of that first week, he took me out, just the two of us. We had dinner at some wildly expensive restaurant. The food was rich and delicious, the atmosphere sinfully romantic. After desert, he pulled me out onto a dance floor and held me close while we moved to the light tunes of a live jazz band.

THE ROCKER THAT SAVORS ME

"I love you, Layla," he whispered against my ear.

Tears stung my eyes. "I love you, too." I felt his smile as he kissed my temple. We continued dancing for several more songs, and then he pulled me out the door and into the Escalade that was already waiting for us outside.

What followed was more intense than our first night together. We didn't go back to his friend Tom's house but to an exclusive hotel just outside of LA. Our suite had candles lit all around the room when we walked inside. Soft music played in the background. Jesse closed the door behind him then lifted me into his arms.

I felt like I was floating as he carried me to the king sized bed. Scattered rose petals scattered across the top, their sweet scent invaded my nose as he lowered me to the mattress. My dress, or rather Lana's dress, disappeared before I realized it, and Jesse was kissing every exposed inch of skin he could get to.

For hours, he savored me. I was weeping by the time we fell into each other's arms. Jesse kissed my hair. "Do you believe me now?" he murmured.

I raised my head, confused. "Believe you about what?"

He smiled. "That I love you."

"Jesse, I believed you the first time you said it." He raised a brow, and I sighed. "Okay, my heart believed you. Now my head does too."

"Good." He yawned, pulled me closer, and we fell asleep locked in each other's arms. Hours later, we made love again and then he told me about his childhood growing up in a trailer park with his band brothers spread out around him and his mother leaving when he was just a toddler. Jesse told me about his father, and I held him close as he described the old man beating him until he was thirteen. By that time, he was bigger than his dad and able to hit back. After he busted the bastard's nose, he never touched his son in violence again. After that Jesse's childhood was pretty normal…

I still got weak kneed every time I thought about that beautiful night. He had made it truly special for us both. In a way it had made this week hard because he wasn't home like he had been the week before. The guys were back in the studio, and I was lonely for the most of the day.

Emmie was busy with work, although she took care of most of it while sitting up in bed now. Nik had forbidden her to get up unless she absolutely had to, and I was in charge of making sure she listened. I was glad that she was distracted by work though because that gave me time to put together my surprise.

On Saturday, I rushed to get through the morning. Lana was helping me, and we were both having a blast getting everything put together. I had told Jesse some of what we had planned, but only because I needed his help with who to call. He hadn't understood a word of what I said, and I had to explain it to him twice before he got it.

By midafternoon we had everything ready, and I was nervous as hell. Jesse had helped me by taking Emmie out for lunch, and they were still gone by the time everyone started arriving. At ten minutes to three, I got a text from him and put everyone in their places. I wasn't sure if surprising a heavily pregnant woman was a good thing, but it couldn't do too much damage.

My heart was racing and my palms were sweaty when I heard Jesse say something that made Emmie laugh. A few moments later, they came out of the house and onto the patio. I held my breath as Emmie took in the sign hanging from the long table loaded with food and presents. Her eyes went huge and she looked at me. "Layla?"

From all directions guests jumped out from their hiding places. "Surprise!" they called and Emmie jumped.

"Oh my Gods!" she whispered, and I was dismayed to see her eyes fill with tears.

"You don't like it?" I asked.

Emmie shook her head, sobbing now. I glanced at Jesse for guidance, but he didn't look like he understood either, so I pulled her close, holding her as much as I could with her stomach between us. "Emmie, I'm sorry. I didn't mean to make you cry." Tears burned my eyes, and I tried to blink them away. One of us crying was enough.

When she had shown me the nursery last week, and I had seen that she only had the bare necessities, I wanted to throw her a baby shower. I wanted my friend to have this special occasion that all mothers should get to have when they were carrying new life inside of them, and I had wanted to be the one to give it to her. I never intended to upset her like this.

"I'm sorry, Emmie. I can ask them all to leave…"

She shook her head again, her arms holding on tight to me while her tears soaked through my top. "No. I'm not mad. I'm…I'm touched. No one has ever…ever…" She broke off, sobbing once again. "I've read all about baby showers and heard the other mothers at the doctor's office gushing over theirs, but I never thought that I would get to have one."

"Oh, Emmie." I kissed her hair, holding her closer.

After a few minutes, she finally pulled away, her face blotchy from crying. Nik, Drake, and Shane—all having been in on my secret as of the day before—stood behind her, but none of them said a word. Emmie gave me a watery smile. "Thank you, Layla. Thank you for this."

Jesse's hand caught mine. "Well, let's get this party started."

For the next two hours, I got to know the people in Emmie's life outside of the guys. I met Alexis Moreitti who was six months pregnant and her husband Jared. Alexis walked with a cane, and I learned that she had been in a car accident. It was a miracle that she was even able to walk, even more so that she was able to carry her child to term. Her husband was nice, and when he looked at her, I could see his love and devotion shining through.

I discovered that Alexis was Gabriella Moreitti's cousin. It wasn't a great discovery either. Gabriella had been invited as well and had come with Axton Cage. It wasn't until half way through the shower that I learned Gabriella and Emmie were anything but friends.

"Why did you tell me to invite her?" I asked Jesse when I realized that Emmie was uncomfortable with the other woman around.

He sighed. "Because I didn't think she would actually show up." He was eating one of the sandwiches that Lana and I had made that morning. From the looks of it, it was one of the chicken salad croissants Lana made from scratch. "Look, Gabriella told Emmie that she hooked up with Nik a while back. It was before Em got pregnant. It was all lies, but Em didn't know that until recently."

I glared up at him. "And yet you still told me to invite her." I had liked talking to the woman, but now I instantly disliked her. No way was I going to like someone that hurt my friend on purpose.

He hung his head and his lower lip pouted out. "I'm sorry, baby."

"Damn." I couldn't stay upset with him when he did things like that. With another glare, I stood on tiptoe to kiss him. "Next time tell me things like this, okay?"

Jesse grinned. "You aren't mad at me?"

"How can I stay mad at you when you give me those big puppy dog eyes and that pouty lip?" I pushed him away when he started to pull me closer. "Go. I have things to do."

He gave me another pouty look, but I was ready for it this time and pushed him off towards his band brothers where they stood talking to Jared Moreitti and Axton Cage. Turning, I started gathering some items for a baby game. There were people spread around the patio and by the pool, and I went around handing out little pencils and paper to everyone who wanted to play.

I glanced Emmie's way and found her laughing with Melissa Shepard and Rich Branson's assistant who had come in his place. I had lucked out there because Jesse had said I had to invite their manager but that Emmie and Rich didn't get along. I was glad to see that Emmie was happy and I was able to give her something that she had wanted but hadn't been able to ask for.

As I finished passing out the game, I stopped by Lana who sat at a table talking to Vince Shepard and Drake. I touched her shoulder to get her attention, and she grinned up at me. "Ready?" she asked.

I nodded and gave her the piece of paper. My sister spent the next thirty minutes being the master of games. Everyone was laughing and Emmie was having so much fun. I watched from the corner as everyone played game after game. Everyone won something, and even Drake was laughing when the games were over.

After the games came the presents, and Emmie struggled through, trying not to cry as she unwrapped each gift. There were clothes, bottles, diapers, blankets, bibs, toys, and a list of other items that brought tears to Emmie's eyes. Lana had even helped the guys pick out a present earlier that morning for them to give to her: a portable swing that played classic lullabies. I waited until she had unwrapped the last gift before I brought out my own present for her.

Jesse had to carry it out for me, and Emmie gave up the struggle and burst into tears when she saw the cradle I had bought her. It was hand crafted with butterflies, bees, and flowers in the carvings. I had known as soon as I saw it that it was perfect for Emmie.

By the time everyone had a piece of cake, I was exhausted. Emmie seemed like she couldn't take anymore. She thanked everyone for coming, and Nik took her up to their room so she could take a nap. Before she went into the house, she hugged me tight and thanked me for making today so special.

"Emmie, you deserved today. I'm glad I was able to give it to you."

Her chin trembled but she turned away before she burst into tears again.

When everyone was gone, the guys helped me clean up. I was thankful for their help because I was dragging by then, although there wasn't all that much to do. The food had all been eaten, everyone loved Lana's sandwiches and the homemade dips. One of was specifically for Emmie's cravings, made with sour-cream, chopped up bacon, and some ranch seasoning. The cake was nearly all gone, and I was glad that I had taken pictures for Emmie before it had been destroyed. She had loved the little pink dress cake with the tiny foot print on the pregnant belly. I had specifically requested that the dress have a girly skull at the top. It had been perfect.

THE ROCKER THAT SAVORS ME

Finally, the patio was clean and I fell into a chair beside of Lana and Lucy. "Today was fun," Lucy told me. She was still munching on some carrot sticks with what was left of Emmie's dip, and I wondered for the millionth time if my baby sister ever got full.

"Yes it was," Jesse agreed as he sat on the edge of my lounger and started rubbing my bare feet. "You girls did a wonderful job. You deserve something special."

I raised a brow at that. "Like what?" I hoped he didn't say something stupid, like a car which was what he had been hinting at for two weeks now, because I didn't have the energy to smack him in the back of his bald head.

He shrugged. "We could go to SeaWorld tomorrow."

Before I could say anything Lucy was already jumping up and down. "Yes! Yes! Yes!" She threw herself into Jesse's arms, and he caught her against him, laughing. "I've never been to SeaWorld before, but I always wanted to go."

"Jesse, that's almost a three hour trip one way," I told him.

His eyes narrowed on me. "You don't want to go to SeaWorld?" Of course he gave me that pouty look that I was unable to say no to.

I sighed. "Fine. SeaWorld it is."

Lucy started dancing around, and Lana was giggling. I guess we were going to SeaWorld with the big bad—totally loveable—rocker.

Chapter 16
Jesse

In the weeks that went by, I fell even more in love with Layla Daniels. Every minute I spent with her was enjoyable, even if all we did was sit holding each other on the couch in front of the television. I also grew closer to Lucy and Lana. Maybe it was because I knew I couldn't have Layla without them, or maybe it was because they were special in their own right. Either way, they attached themselves to my heart in an irreversible way. When I thought of my future, I couldn't imagine it without any one of them.

It was scary to have my heart triple in size over the course of a month. I went from only loving Emmie and my band brothers to loving three more, but I didn't run from it. If anything, I embraced it and it only made me more determined. With Emmie's help, everything was coming along smoothly. All I had to do was talk to Layla about it.

I couldn't do it tonight though. My buddy Tom was home now, and he had called to invite me and the guys to a party at his house. Nik didn't want to go because Emmie was just two weeks away from her scheduled C-section and was feeling more miserable by the day. I had planned on taking Layla out somewhere special and talking to her, but Tom had guilt-tripped me into attending.

Layla decided to go with me, which I was thankful for. I in no way wanted to attend one of Tom's parties without Layla, not with all those girls hanging around. There was no chance that I would cheat on her, but if she found out what those parties were like without being there with me, I was sure that it would have caused trouble.

Lana was staying home with Lucy, and Drake had planned on staying in with her. The weekend before, Drake had pulled one of Layla's tricks and threw Lana a surprise birthday party. I had been relieved that he had gotten her a new car because seriously Layla's old one had broken down twice the week before. I had helped pick it out, which was a plus, because both women were beyond crazy mad when Drake gifted Lana with the keys to the Audi.

The white Audi A6 was one of the top rated safest cars available. When Layla had heard that, she calmed down a little. It had taken lots of pleading on Drakes part for Lana to accept the car. Finally, it was Emmie who had solved the problem by taking out the car's paper work and giving it to Lana. "It's yours. Your name is on the paper work. Take the car and stop tormenting him!" Lana took it without any further arguing. We had all learned over the last week or so not to get Emmie too upset. The littlest things could send her into a rage or worse...sobbing.

I picked Layla up at eight so we could go to the party. She looked gorgeous in a silver top that was tight across her chest and black leggings paired with the boots she had worn on our first date. I was tempted to skip the party and take her somewhere we could spend the night getting lost in each other.

Instead, I had settled on a deep kiss before I put her into the passenger seat of the SUV. "I love you," I told her before I closed the door and was rewarded with one of her sexy little smiles.

When we got to Tom's, I wasn't surprised to see people were already spilling out of the house. Some were people from the rock world that I had met over the years. Most were girls there to see whose bed they could get into that night. Layla shook her head as we walked in, obviously already not liking the scene around us.

I gave her hand a reassuring squeeze as I pulled her through the crowded mansion looking for my old buddy. Along the way, I passed Shane and Layla gave a disgusted grunt when she saw that he had two girls sitting on his lap making out. I pulled her closer. "This is tame for Shane," I reminded her. In the time that we had been together, we had come across Shane in worse scenes than this.

"It's still hard to witness," she muttered, and I had to agree.

Axton came up to us. It looked like he and Gabriella were off again because he wasn't fighting off the girls like he normally would when the two were together. I think I preferred him with Gabriella than without. I could tell he was wasted, which was the only reason I didn't smash my friend's face in when he started hitting on Layla.

By ten, I still hadn't found Tom. Layla excused herself and went off to find a free bathroom. I was tired of looking for the old rocker and decided that as soon as Layla got back from the bathroom we were going home.

That thought had no more crossed my mind when I saw Layla appear at the top of the stairs. I looked up, hoping to catch her eye to let her know we were leaving when everything went to hell…

Layla

I pushed my way through the crowd. The place looked different compared to when I was last here. Then, I had felt so happy having just spent the night in the arms of the man I'd fallen in love with. Now, I felt almost dirty watching all the girls as they practically whored themselves out so they could say they had had sex with some rocker, or whatever it was that those types of girls got out of it. It reminded me of my childhood and how my mother would go to parties just like this, leaving me in the car while she spent hours inside some stranger's house.

After seeing Shane, a man I had grown to love as a brother, making out with not one, not two, but three different women tonight, I had a sick feeling in my stomach that wouldn't go away. I hurried up in the powder room, hoping that I could convince Jesse to take me home soon.

When I came out of the bathroom on the second floor, it was to find a couple making out against the wall by the door. It startled me because they hadn't been there when I had gone in just a few minutes ago. As I moved to walk past them, I happened to take a closer look at them and was unable to contain my startled gasp.

No way! There was absolutely no way I was seeing this. Life was not that cruel! It was not that fucked up! Oh shit. Oh shit. Oh. Shit!

The couple heard my gasp and the man raised his head. Chocolate brown eyes narrowed on me when they met my gaze. His eyes were blood shot, and I knew he had to be drunk, or high,

THE ROCKER THAT SAVORS ME

or both. That didn't stop the recognition I saw cross his face or the way those narrowed eyes turned into a cold glare.

He pushed the girl away from him, and I was sickened to see that she wasn't much older than Lana. What the hell did that little girl see in a sixty year old man? "What the fuck are *you* doing here?" he demanded.

I swallowed my revulsion and returned his glare. "I'm here with my boyfriend."

Tommy Kirkman sneered down at me. "What idiot would be stupid enough to get involved with you? Some sap with more money than brains obviously."

Rage burned in my veins, and I clenched my hands into fists so I wouldn't be tempted to smack the jackass. "Well, it's nice to see you haven't changed much over the years. Still the same slime ball, horn dog you always were. Tell me, is she legal?"

"Trust me, I've learned my lesson." He took a step closer to me, and I almost took a step back. I wasn't scared of this man. I would never be scared of him. All he was now was a washed up rocker. He was lucky enough to have invested his money well over the years because he didn't have that same big money coming in on a regular basis now that his career was over.

"What? You check their IDs before you screw them?" I asked, tossing my hair over my shoulder. "Or do you make them bring their birth certificates just in case? Does the guy that lives here know that he has a nasty old man running around trying to bed all the little girls?" Even as the words left me, the truth hit me, and I felt all the color drain from my face.

Tom…Tommy. Yeah, I was definitely on slow motion tonight in the brain department. I should have put it together by now, but I didn't let thoughts of this creep enter my mind all that often. Now that I had realized my mistake, I knew that my heart was about to be shattered into a million pieces.

A strong hand touched my arm, and I jerked. Jesse frowned at my reaction, but I looked away, avoiding his eyes. "What's wrong?" he demanded. When I didn't answer, his eyes moved to his friend. "Tom?"

THE ROCKER THAT SAVORS ME

I felt Tommy stiffening. "You?" he asked, his voice rising. "You are with her?"

"What's going on here, Tom?" He spoke with more force now. "You and my girl not hitting it off?"

I felt bile rising in the back of my throat, but I took several deep breaths to keep it down. I wanted to hit a rewind button and have this night never happen. If I didn't know that Tommy Kirkman was the great man that Jesse had told me so much about I could ignore the rest. I could keep from shattering. I wouldn't have to leave him or Emmie or the guys.

But there wasn't a rewind button or even a pause button so I could soak in the man I loved one last time before I walked away from him forever…

"How did you get involved with her?" Tommy demanded, stepping closer to Jesse.

Jesse seemed to grow bigger before my eyes. "What's it to you?" he asked in a tone that I had never heard him use before. It was cold and full of steel, and I chanced a glance at him to see that his eyes were changing by the second.

"Jesse…" I started to touch him, but Tommy grabbed my arm and jerked me away from him.

I cried out, his hold on my arm so tight it would leave bruises. "You don't get to touch him," Tommy snarled at me, his face getting so close to mine the stench of whiskey and smoke on his breath made me gag. "He's too good for the likes of you!"

I flinched, his words just as painful as his touch. I hated him, hated him to my very soul, and yet a part of me loved him too. A tiny little part of me would always crave his love and acceptance. Didn't all daughters want that from their fathers?

Tommy released me so quickly I wasn't sure what was going on. I raised my head to find Jesse pinning him against the wall, his eyes full of white hot rage. "You touch her like that again, and I will make you swallow teeth!" he roared at his old friend.

Tommy stared up at the drummer with a dazed look in his chocolate brown eyes. "You would turn on me over a girl like her? Over some little whore that…" He didn't get to finish what he was going to say. Jesse's fist connected with his jaw making his head snap back, and I wasn't sure if Jesse had followed through with his threat or not because blood gathered in the corner of Tommy's mouth.

"You don't get to talk about her like that either!" Jesse shouted at him.

Someone turned the music off, making the place unusually quiet. I glanced over my shoulder to see all eyes were on us. Fuck! I did not need this now. I grabbed Jesse's arm. "Jess, please. Just take me home," I pleaded.

"Not until he tells you he's sorry." Jesse tightened his hold on Tommy's shirt. "Tell her."

Tommy turned his head and spit right at my feet. "Fuck off."

Tears gathered in my eyes, but I refused to let him see. "I don't need an apology. Just take me home."

"Layla…"

"Layla!"

My head snapped around at the sound of Lana's voice. I didn't know how she knew I needed her, but I didn't question it; I was too glad to see my sister. She was running through the doorway with Drake right behind her. "Layla, let's go," she commanded.

I released my hold on Jesse's arm. She ran up the stairs and took hold of my arms, inspecting me as if she was scared I had lost a limb or something. "Are you okay?" she demanded, shooting Tommy a vile glare.

"I'm fine," I whispered. "Can…Can you take me home?"

"Of course." She pulled me into her side, and I didn't look back as she led me away. Drake fell into step behind us. I kept my eyes down as I passed through the crowd of partiers. I couldn't bring myself to hold up my head like I had the right to. No one would believe anything but what Tommy Kirkman told them anyway.

"Layla!" Jesse had followed us out of the house, but he stopped me when I went to get into Lana's car. "Layla, what the fuck just happened in there?" His rage hadn't dimmed at all. If anything, he looked even angrier. "How do you know Tom?" he demanded.

THE ROCKER THAT SAVORS ME

I closed my eyes, knowing what he suspected. It was what everyone in that room suspected. That I was some out casted lover of the great Tommy Kirkman. "I can't tell you." I whispered.

"Why the fuck not?" He yelled.

"Because I signed a nondisclosure form when I was sixteen!" I yelled back at him. "I can't tell anyone anything!"

"You might not be able to, but I sure as hell can," Lana said, getting between me and Jesse. She didn't even blink as she glared up at him. "Stop looking at my sister like that, Jesse Thornton! She didn't do anything wrong."

"Then why isn't she talking?" He tried to push her out of his way so he could get to me, but she didn't budge. "Move, Lana!" He didn't try to touch her, but when she refused to budge, he started to move around her. Drake moved behind Lana, and I was thankful for the added wall of flesh that separated me from Jesse.

"No. Fuck you!" Lana shoved him hard, and surprisingly, he moved back a few steps. "You're thinking the worst of her right now. I can see the wheels turning in that fucked up rocker world mentality that you have. My sister is better than that. She is better than *you*. And she's sure as fuck better than her fuck faced father."

I swallowed hard, not caring that Lana was using words I had asked her not to. My heart shattered because I had seen what Jesse was thinking too, and it had gone down the dirty route. I opened the door to Lana's car and got in.

This was over. I was done. Turned out that Jesse Thornton was exactly who I had first thought he was.

THE ROCKER THAT SAVORS ME

Chapter 17
Layla

I felt like I was in a daze the entire trip back to Malibu. Lana drove quickly but carefully and got us home in record time. No one spoke. Lana knew that I wasn't ready to talk about it, and Drake, who was sitting in the back, didn't say a word.

When we pulled into the driveway, I got out of the car and walked to the guesthouse with my head down. I heard Drake murmuring something to Lana but didn't care one way or another what he was saying. I was numb. Cold. This night was a disaster, and I wished I had never gotten out of bed that morning.

When I opened the door to the guesthouse, Nik jumped to his feet. His presence here surprised me. "What are you doing here?" I asked, my voice sounding hoarse.

"Drake asked me to keep an eye on Lucy. She was sleeping when they left and hasn't woken up since." He took a step towards me, looking concerned. "Layla, are you okay?" He glanced behind me. "Where's Jesse?"

I shrugged. "Probably still at Tommy's." I didn't care where he was right now as long as he wasn't near me. I swallowed hard. "Thanks for watching Lucy, but do you mind going home now? I...I'm not very good company."

"Did you and Jesse have a fight?"

"Something like that." I kicked off my boots and dropped down on the couch. Lana walked in through the still open door with Drake behind her like always. There was tension radiating from him, and I knew it was because of me. Was he scared I was going to pack up and take Lana far away from him? Trust me, the thought had crossed my mind more than once on the drive home.

But I wasn't going to run away. I refused to give up Emmie and the life that my sisters and I had here just because I had been stupid enough to fall for a guy that would think the worst of me. I wasn't going anywhere unless Emmie, and only Emmie, asked me to leave. "Go home, guys."

"Layla..." Drake gave me an almost pleading look. "Call me before you decide anything crazy, okay? Don't run." His eyes went to Lana who stood just a few feet in front of him. *Don't take her away from me*, his eyes seemed to say.

"I'm not running," I assured him and saw his shoulders noticeably relax. "But you need to go. I'm not strong enough to deal with you here right now."

Nik still stood over me, frowning. "Tell me what happened, Layla. Maybe I can help."

I glared up at him. "You can't help. Nothing you say or do will fix what happened tonight. Nothing, not even a time machine could change any of it. Not unless you have a way of extracting DNA from someone's gene pool."

He only looked more confused now. "Did you and Jesse break up?"

"Oh, yeah. We definitely broke up," I told him with a laugh that held little humor.

Nik opened his mouth to say something, but Drake stopped him. "Let's go, bro. She just needs some time to get tonight straight in her head." Nik sighed but nodded, and I was relieved when both rockers left without another word.

Once the door was shut behind them, Lana dropped down beside me on the sofa and without a word, pulled me into her arms. Like a child, I buried my face in her hair and held on as the tears fell freely. My past had come back to bite me in a big way…

My mother, Lydia, had only been sixteen when she met Tommy Kirkman. Sixteen to his thirty-five. Of course she hadn't told him that she was only sixteen. I was sure that she hadn't even been a virgin when she had willingly climbed into the rocker's bed. She had meant to get pregnant. It was all part of her plan to become a rocker's wife or at least his play thing for longer than a night.

Tommy had picked up and moved on the next day, but Lydia had made sure that he knew that she was pregnant. When I was born, a court ordered paternity test was done, and Tommy had forked over some big time money but made sure that my mother knew that he wanted nothing to do with me. She had been disappointed that I wasn't enough to keep the rock star on a leash

THE ROCKER THAT SAVORS ME

for at least a little while, but the money he had shelled out had been enough to console her.

I hadn't really thought about the man that was my father growing up. I had known who he was from the time I was old enough to ask about him. It wasn't until my mother kicked me out when I was sixteen that I tried to contact him.

I had nowhere to go, was living in a shelter and barely getting anything to eat. I had been desperate, so I went to one of his concerts. It hadn't been easy, but somehow I managed to sneak onto his tour bus and waited for him. He had been high on the adrenaline from his performance and maybe something stronger, but he hadn't been so stoned that he didn't understand who I was when I told him I was his daughter.

Tommy Kirkman had been less than pleased to see me. I didn't have a copy of my birth certificate to show as proof, but I didn't really need one. I might have looked a little like my mother, but I had more of my father in me. My chocolate brown eyes, the rich cinnamon color of my hair, the angle of my chin and the shape of my nose—that was all Tommy.

"So what do you want?" he had snarled after I told him who I was.

"I...My mom threw me out. I don't have anywhere to go," I told him, putting my pride aside because I had nothing left.

"That's your problem." He moved around the bus until he found a half empty bottle of whiskey. He pulled the top off and started drinking directly from the bottle. "That settlement I gave your slut mother was to make you go away. I signed over all my rights, and she got her money."

"But..." I knew I was fighting for a lost cause. He wasn't going to help me. Not unless... "I'll sell my story to the papers. I'm sure that all your fans would love to read about your bastard in the gossip pages." Not to mention I was likely to get a good price for selling my story. "And wouldn't the world like hearing how you got a sixteen year old pregnant?" Maybe it was the truth, or maybe I was just trying to bluff him into helping me out. I wasn't sure. I could never really know. I was a scared, desperate girl then, but I left with that threat ringing between us.

THE ROCKER THAT SAVORS ME

The next day I met Zeke and he took me in, and I forgot about the threat I had made to Tommy.

So it came as a surprise when two weeks later a stuffy looking lawyer had knocked on Zeke's door. He worked for Tommy Kirkman, and he had something for me. A check for five thousand dollars if I signed the nondisclosure, keeping me from ever telling anyone about who Tommy was to me. It wasn't much, not considering the amount he had given my mother to keep her mouth shut, but I didn't care. I was done with Tommy. I didn't need him. I had someone that cared about me now, someone who worried if I was actually eating. I took the money and signed the nondisclosure, never thinking I would ever have to explain myself to anyone where Tommy Kirkman was concerned...

"Layla!"

My head jerked up and I wiped at my tear stained face. Jesse was outside pounding on the front door. "Layla, open up and talk to me!" He sounded just as angry as he had back at the party. Some of my numbness started to fade, and before I could think better of it, I was on my feet and across the living room pulling open the door.

Jesse

Father.

Father?

Father!

Lana's last words kept echoing in my head. Layla was Tom's daughter. It was a relief. The first thing that had crossed my mind was...

"Fuck!" I scrubbed my hands across my face. "Fuck!" The look on Layla's face as I had yelled at her came back to haunt me. Now that my rage, my jealousy at thinking that my friend had touched Layla in any way, was evaporating, my gut filled with dread and fear. I had assumed the worst when I should have known immediately that my Layla wasn't like other women. She hated rockers and would have never have been involved with one.

I was the exception. I knew that I was one lucky bastard that she had given me her heart. I had no excuse for the way I behaved, unless you counted the fact that I had never been jealous in my life until tonight. It wasn't a good feeling, and I hadn't known how to handle it, so I took it out on the woman I loved. And now I might have lost her…

My heart contracted painfully, and I pulled the keys from my jeans pocket as I turned towards where I had parked the Escalade.

Before I had gone more than a few feet, I saw the three men coming towards me. The lights from the house and the lamps outside gave me more than enough light to see that Tom wasn't happy. The two goons that acted as his personal body guards had their jaws set, and I knew what was coming before my old friend even opened his mouth.

"Nice punch there, Jesse." Tom rubbed his hand across his already swollen jaw. "That girl must be good on her knees because I have never known you to…" He broke off abruptly when I took a menacing step in his direction.

"You don't talk about her like that. Ever!" I snarled at the guy I had once considered a good friend. "I'm going to marry *that girl*." If she would still have me. If I hadn't just screwed up everything.

Tom snorted. "Why would you do that? She's just after what she can get from you. All that rocker money, just like her mother. As soon as she gets what she wants, you will be history, my friend."

"You know nothing about her. How could you? You haven't had anything to do with Layla her whole life so don't tell me what you think you know about your daughter, old man." I watched Tom's eyes darken when I said the word *daughter*.

"She's no daughter of mine. I don't care what those blood tests said. She's not mine." He turned to go back into the house, but the goons stood in the same place. "It was good knowing you, Jesse," Tom called over his shoulder, laughing in a sickeningly humorous way that made me grit my teeth.

I didn't take my eyes off the old rocker as he made his way into the house. If he thought that two over muscled wannabe thugs were going to end me, he had another think coming. I had spent

THE ROCKER THAT SAVORS ME

my life fighting with odds bigger than this against me. I could handle these two without breaking a sweat...

The first punch came from behind, and I fell to my knees. A third goon had come around from behind. I should have known better. Tom liked to fight dirty. Hadn't I seen just that the few times we had gotten into bar fights all those years ago?

Muttering a curse, I rolled to my side as one of the other goons swung his foot and tried to connect with my ribs. He just barely missed me, and I was thankful for my quick reflexes. When I got to my feet, the last goon was waiting on me, and I ducked to escape his right hook, countering it with a punch to his mouth as I side stepped him.

Strong arms caught mine from behind, holding me in place. I struggled, realizing that a fourth goon had come to join our little party. The other three took advantage of having me restrained and started taking turns using me as a punching bag. The air was knocked out of me by the first guy, making me double over to suck in oxygen.

It wasn't much of a fight that was for sure. Not when I was unable to defend myself against four steroid junkies. A punch from the guy to my right made my head snap back, and I tasted blood as my teeth snapped together and I bit my tongue. Fuck, that hurt!

"Jesse!"

Shane! I raised my head and saw my band brother just as the guy to my left started in on my kidneys.

"Axton!" Shane shouted. "Get out here!"

"What the fuck man..." Axton broke off when he saw what was going on, and then I heard running feet as they hurried to help me. The guys to my right were tackled to the ground, and I heard them grunting as my friends used their fists to keep them down.

The guy still holding me tightened his arms. The goon that had been having so much fun trying to rupture my kidney wasn't deterred by the arrival of my help. If anything, he seemed more into it with the sounds of his co-workers getting the shit beat out of them behind him. He got cocky and eased up on me just a little.

That was all I needed. I kicked with my right leg and connected with the fucker's favorite man part. I watched in satisfaction as the muscle man clutched his junk. His face turned an unnatural shade of purple, and he fell to his knees. He was out of the game, not recovering from the force of my kick any time soon.

The goon behind me let up on his grip, and I used my head to knock him back. My shaved head connected with his nose, and I felt something warm and wet gushing down my neck. The guy fell back taking me with him since he hadn't let go of me yet. I pushed away from him as soon as I was on the ground. Getting to my feet, I kicked him in the ribs on my way to help Axton.

Axton, on a good night, could fight with the best of them, but tonight he was drunk off his ass. Any help that he might have thought he was giving me had only been momentarily because now the goon had him pinned to the ground, hitting him anywhere and everywhere. Muttering a curse, I pushed the guy off my friend and kicked the goon in the gut while he was still down.

Behind me Shane was getting to his feet. When I turned to look at him, I saw that his lip was bleeding but otherwise he seemed fine. "What the hell just went down out here?" he demanded, slightly out of breath.

I blew out a long sigh. "It's a long story." I told him as I helped Axton to his feet.

"Where's Layla? Is she okay?"

My gut clenched. "She went home. We…" I muttered a curse under my breath. "Look, let's just go home. I need to talk to Layla."

"You go." Shane took hold of the unsteady Axton, pulling the rocker's arm over his shoulder to better guide him. "I'm going to take Ax home. He's wasted."

I helped Shane get him into his car before heading back to Malibu. The drive was long, and I was really starting to feel the effects of the beating I had just taken. All the way home I kept praying to whoever would listen that Layla wasn't already gone. She had plenty of time to pack up a few things and get her sisters out of the guesthouse. I kept telling myself that Drake wouldn't let that happen, that he wouldn't just let Layla take Lana away from him like that.

THE ROCKER THAT SAVORS ME

But my heart told me that if it came down to it, Drake would go with them. If he had to choose between Lana and anything—anything—it would always be Lana. Me, Emmie, the guys? We came in second to her now, and that was the way it should be.

That was the way it was for me where Layla was concerned. I had never thought it was possible, but I loved Layla more than I loved Emmie. It was a different love I felt for both of them, but Layla was the queen of my heart. If I had to choose between the two—and I prayed that I never had to because it would kill me—I would pick Layla hands down.

I was relieved to find Lana's car still in the driveway when I pulled in. The lights in the big house were all off, but there were a few still on in the guesthouse. I wanted to run, but the pain in my sides wouldn't let me. By the time I got to the front door, I was breathing hard, the pain gripping me in a bad way, making me wonder if that fucker had done some internal damage.

With what felt like the last of my strength, I pounded on the door of the guesthouse. "Layla!" I shouted. "Layla, open up and talk to me." I pounded again.

Without warning, the door opened and I was rewarded with the sight of my goddess standing in the doorway. Gods, she was beautiful when she was mad. I smiled despite the pain. I loved her so much my chest ached.

"Oh my God!" Layla cried. "What happened?" she demanded, all signs of anger gone in the face of the evidence of the little party I had been invited to after she had left.

"Tom didn't like me punching him, so he had his bodyguards take care of me." I leaned against the doorframe, feeling weak. "Can I come in? I don't know how much longer I can stand on my own?"

Her eyes widened. "Fuck, Jesse." She stepped back to let me pass. Relieved that she was letting me in, I took a step inside and nearly fell on my face. She let out a little cry and reached for me. "Jesus, Jess!" She tried to catch me, but I was too much for her and she went crashing to the floor with me.

THE ROCKER THAT SAVORS ME

"Layla?" Lana's concerned voice came from somewhere behind us. "What..? Jesse, there's blood all over your head and neck!"

I grimaced. "Not mine," I assured her.

"Then who the hell does it belong too?" Layla demanded, touching a trembling hand to my head. "Your shirt is soaked with it, Jesse."

"One of Tom's boys. I broke his nose when I head butted him." Unable to stand, I turned over and lay there on my back. This sucked. I was probably going to have to go to the hospital. I didn't want to go, especially when there was so much I needed to talk to Layla about.

She was still lying on the floor beside me, and I reached for her, pulling her across my chest. She looked worried and tears were making her big chocolate eyes glittery. "Lana, call Drake. Tell him to bring Nik," Layla told her sister. "We have to get him to the hospital." It tore me up inside to hear the quiver in her voice.

"Will you go with me?" I asked, stroking my fingers through her hair. God, I was hurting, but I wasn't about to stop touching her!

"Of course I'm coming with you." She was running her hands over me, trying to judge just how damaged I was. "Where does it hurt the most?"

"I think one of them got my kidney pretty good."

"How many were there?" Lana asked, crouching down beside of us. "Because you look like they really fucked you up."

"Four," I told her honestly. "One of them held me while the others took turns." Layla's eyes filled with horror, and I grimaced, hating that I had put those images in her head.

"Lana!" Drake was running and I looked up just as he and Nik stopped in the doorway of the guesthouse.

"Fuck!" Nik exclaimed. "Oh, shit!" He crouched down beside of Lana. "Dude, what happened?"

I was already tired of telling the story. I gave them a quick recap and just lay there with my eyes closed, using what energy I had left to play with Layla's hair. As long as I was touching her, I was okay. The pain was manageable.

THE ROCKER THAT SAVORS ME

"Help me get him to the Escalade," Layla urged the guys. She moved away from me to let Nik and Drake on either side of me, and I protested. "Hush. I'm right here."

Between the two of them, they got me to the Escalade, and I stretched out in the backseat. Was it bad that I felt like puking? Because I suddenly felt the need to do just that. Drake jumped into the driver's seat, and Layla got in the back with me. I had to hold my head up long enough to let her sit down, but then I felt utter relief as I put my head in her lap.

Trembling fingers skimmed over my swollen face. My eye was tender, and I figured it was a rainbow of colors by now. My lips hurt and my jaw ached, but none of that pain could compete with the pain coming from my left side. "I'm sorry, Jesse," Layla whispered, touching the blood on my chin.

"I'm the one that's sorry, baby." I caught her fingers and kissed each one. "I went a little crazy tonight. My only excuse is that I was jealous, and that's a new emotion for me. I've never experienced anything like what I have with you. It's terrifying at times."

Her smile was all quivery, and I wanted to erase this night from both our minds. "It scares me too. The way I love you is more intense than anything I've ever felt before."

"Can you forgive me for thinking the worst?" If she didn't forgive me I didn't know what I was going to do. Without her, my future was a big, blank void.

"I forgave you as soon as I realized you were hurt." She sighed. "I won't lie. It hurt that you thought I would have been with Tommy, but I understand your jealousy. If our places were reversed, I would have gone over the top too. I'm crazy obsessed with you."

I grinned. "Me too, babe."

Her fingers stroked over my head. If I hadn't been in so much pain, I was sure it would have made me hard just as it always did when she touched me like this, but for now I was dead in that department. Still, it made my heart race, and I tugged on her hair until she lowered her head and skimmed her lips over mine. "I love you, Layla."

THE ROCKER THAT SAVORS ME

"I love you, too."

THE ROCKER THAT SAVORS ME

Chapter 18
Layla

We were at the hospital all night. Doctors came and went, only to have more doctors come and go. After X-rays, CT scans, blood work, and a urine sample was collected, they determined that Jesse had a severely bruised left kidney and would have to spend the night for observations. Thankfully, he didn't have blood in his urine and it was only after the urologist on call had come in to explain the severity of what that possibility could mean did I understand that Jesse had been very lucky.

Drake left at dawn, but I stayed. I couldn't leave him. I watched over him while he slept, thanks to the painkillers that they fed into his IV. He looked peaceful even with his face all swollen and varying shades of blue, purple, and black.

I had been scared last night before he had come home. Scared that he wasn't going to want me anymore. Scared that Tommy was going to fill his head with all kinds of sick things that would make him hate me. That fear had only made the hurt worse last night. But when I had opened that door and saw my battered love standing on the other side, everything else didn't matter anymore.

I just wanted to kiss it all better and have him hold onto me forever…

Around nine, the doctor came in and told Jesse he could go home. He was ordered to rest. I was told to make sure Jesse was going to the bathroom regularly and what to watch for in case he needed to come back. I paid extra attention, afraid I would miss something important.

Shane showed up to take us home. When we returned to the beach house, Emmie met us at the door. She was pale and an emotional wreck. Nik hadn't told her anything until Shane had left to pick us up. I tried to soothe her, but she was off the walls today. She went from crying to sobbing to pissed off in the blink of an eye and you never knew which was coming next.

Right now, she was pacing in the living room, shooting Jesse glares from time to time as she muttered under her breath. I sat there watching her while I stroked my fingers over the stubble on

Jesse's head as he lay there trying to relax. He was pale under the rainbow of bruises on his face. The pain killers they had prescribed for him were making him loopy, but they were also making him nauseous too.

"I can't believe you didn't know that Tommy Kirkman was her father!"

My head snapped up at Emmie's sudden outburst. She was pacing still—well waddling. Her feet were swollen and the baby was so low that Emmie walked bowlegged most of the time. She was so cute to look at, but right now I was so stunned by my friend's tirade that I didn't see the cuteness.

Jesse frowned up at her. "You mean you did?"

"Of course I knew." She stopped to glare down at him. "I've known since the first week she started working here." Her eyes went to me, and I saw an apology in their green depths. "I had to do a background check on you, Layla. I know I should have told you, but I needed to know if there was anything that might hurt Jesse. Even then, I knew he was crazy about you…"

I gave her a small smile. "It's okay. I understand." I would have done the same in her position. Jesse and the guys were her family, and she wanted to protect them just as much as I wanted to protect Lana and Lucy.

"Why didn't you tell me?" Jesse demanded, sitting up.

"Because I didn't think it mattered. So she's Tommy's daughter? Who the fuck cares? That doesn't change who she is." Emmie brushed the hair out of her eyes. "And I figured that if she wasn't going to tell us then there was a good reason."

"But…"

Emmie climbed onto his lap and wrapped her arms around his neck. "I love you. You know that you and Drake and Shane mean the world to me. But Layla has grabbed onto my heart too. The minute you said you loved her, she became partial owner of my heart too."

I bit my lip as tears burned my eyes.

"So when I got the report back on her, my loyalties were split. I wasn't going to betray her by telling you all her secrets. That was between you and her. If she told you, then fine. If she didn't, that was fine too. But I couldn't be the one to tell you. Still, I'm surprised that you couldn't see she was Tommy's daughter. Fuck, Jesse. She looks so much like him."

I grimaced, not sure that was a complement or not. "I didn't say anything because Tommy means nothing to me," I told them. "He rarely crosses my mind. To me, he isn't my father." I knew that legally I wasn't supposed to say anything about Tommy to anyone, but these were my friends. If I couldn't trust them to keep my secrets, then I couldn't trust anyone. That had been my mistake to begin with. I should have told Jesse about my dad weeks ago when he told me about his own childhood.

"No, he isn't," Emmie agreed. "He's just a pile of shit taking up space. The first time I met him I was seventeen and he tried to seduce me."

Three heads snapped up at that. Shane was sitting on the other end of the sectional with Nik. "The fuck you say!" Nik exploded. "You never told me that."

She rolled her eyes. "He was your friend. You all had nothing but good things to say about the great Tommy Kirkman. I didn't want to spoil your image of him."

"I'm going to gut him," Nik muttered.

"Stab him a few times for me, babe." Emmie winked at him.

After that, the atmosphere in the house went back to normal. Emmie's emotions evened out, and we spent the rest of the day watching television. Lucy came over and sat with Jesse after lunch. I hadn't wanted her to see him all beaten up, but she was just as worried about him as I was. In the last few weeks, he had become special to her. He was something that she had never had before, a father figure that spoiled her rotten.

She sat on his lap and cuddled with him, kissing a boo-boo from time to time. Jesse held me close to his side, and I was content. It felt like the three of us were a family.

The next week passed by in a blur. Saturday night was put behind us, and I was happy to be moving forward. Jesse's bruises started to fade, and his face got back to the same sinful sexiness I loved so much. The guys stayed home. Since Jesse couldn't go into the studio, they took the week off.

THE ROCKER THAT SAVORS ME

I loved having him around during the day. It made work so much more interesting. I also enjoyed having the other guys around too. Drake and I had gotten close over the last few weeks. I understood him better now and didn't ever question his feelings towards my sister anymore. Drake was a good man, and I would trust him with Lana's life. I liked spending time with Shane and Nik too.

It felt like we were all just one big family, and I loved every minute of it.

...Emmie...

I woke to an empty bed. That made me particularly sad, and I snuggled Nik's pillow close for a few minutes before forcing myself to get out of bed. I had gotten spoiled the week before. Having Nik home and all to myself—getting to sleep with him until noon—had been my own personal paradise.

This week he was back at the studio. He wanted to get as many songs recorded as possible before I went in to have my scheduled C-section next week. So far there was a list of songs a mile long that they had already gotten down, but I knew that only a fraction of them would make the new album. It just depended on how the label wanted to go. What direction they thought the new material should go in. Nik and the guys had the final say so on what they put on there, but the big guys in suits would have a bigger say in it all.

Missing Nik, I got up and showered. I was feeling really good today. Better than I had in what felt like a long time. This last trimester had kicked my ass that was for sure!

Once I was clean, I got out and wrapped a towel around myself. My stomach peeked through, and I grinned at myself in the mirror. I kind of liked the pregnant belly, despite the ugly stretch marks I had to go along with it.

After I was dressed, I went around the bedroom straightening up the room. Tossing Nik's underwear in the hamper, I found that I couldn't stand the sight of my bathroom so disorganized. Before I knew what I was doing, I had the bathroom looking like new.

THE ROCKER THAT SAVORS ME

Standing up from having scrubbed the tub, I felt a small pinch in my lower back. Grimacing, I put the cleaning supplies back under the sink, but I still felt restless. The urge to clean was almost overwhelming. After I washed my hands, I went downstairs to see if Layla needed help with anything.

My friend was a dream when it came to keeping my house clean. The place shined. Especially the kitchen, which was where I found Layla. She was scrubbing the counters when I walked in. Seeing me, she grinned. "Hey, sleepyhead. Enjoy your chance to sleep in?"

I smiled back. "It was nice, but I missed Nik. You don't have to do my bathroom today, by the way. I took care of that for you. "

The grin on Layla's face dimmed. "You were cleaning?"

I shrugged. "Yeah. I just felt this need to clean… Why are you looking at me like that?" Layla was frowning at me with concern.

"Emmie, you're nesting."

"Oh." I read about that in all those books Nik and I had bought. The need to get the "nest" ready before the baby showed up. There was some old wives' tale about it being a sign that the baby was on its way. "I guess I am nesting. I feel kind of restless. Is there anything left to clean?"

"No!" Layla tossed her rag in the sink and washed her hands. "I'm going to make you something to eat, and you are going to go sit on the sectional. You're going to watch television and not move unless you have to."

Her concern touched me, but I actually had energy for the first time in weeks. I wasn't wasting it sitting around. "Relax, Layla. I want to do something." She was already getting the bacon out of the fridge. "What would you like for breakfast?"

I glanced at the clock on the stove. "It's too late for breakfast. How about a sandwich? Will you eat with me?" I loved getting to have a quiet meal with Layla. Even when we didn't talk, it was nice just to be around her.

"Will you promise to rest afterward?"

I sighed. "I really don't want to."

Her chocolate brown eyes narrowed on me. "I'm not Jesse. That little pouty thing doesn't work on me."

THE ROCKER THAT SAVORS ME

I laughed. I hadn't even realized that I was pouting. "Oh, Layla. I'm so happy that you came into our lives."

For the next half an hour, we sat at the island and shared lunch. It was crazy how quickly I had included her in our family, even more so that I couldn't imagine my family without her or her sisters. I was glad that Jesse was able to find happiness with someone as loving and full of life as Layla, someone who didn't put up with his shit…Or mine.

"Okay, I'm going to go watch television now." I grinned as I stood up. "Want to join me?"

She grimaced. "I have a load of clothes in the dryer. Shane has more clothes than Lana."

I laughed. Shane was worse than any girl when it came to clothes. He was the only one of my guys that I didn't have to shop for. "Good luck with that."

Layla stuck her tongue out at me. "Thanks!"

Still laughing, I turned around and made my way out of the kitchen. Two steps and I stopped. There was a sudden pressure between my legs. Just as suddenly it was gone. I didn't think anything of it until I felt my panties getting soaked. When I realized what was happening fear overtook me and I screamed.

"Oh. FUCK!" Layla exclaimed.

Chapter 19
Jesse

"I can't believe you just said that, dude!" I wiped my mouth with my napkin and tossed a fry at Shane. He had been telling crazy, funny jokes from the time we had sat down for lunch. Already, Nik had spit soda out his nose, and I was sure that Shane was determined to make us all do the same.

"What?" Shane grinned. "It's true."

Drake snorted. "How do you know? Oh, wait. I don't want to know." He shook his head, making his hair fall in his face as he gave his younger brother a disgusted yet amused glare. "I don't need to know how you know a woman can do that!"

I was still laughing when my phone buzzed, and I pulled it out of my back pocket to see Layla's gorgeous face smiling back at me. "Hey, baby," I greeted.

There was a pause on the line and for some reason my heart tensed. "Layla?"

There were muttered curses in the background before Layla's voice came clearly through. "Jesse, where are you?" she demanded, sounding anxious and out of breath.

"Having lunch with the guys. What's going on?" I thought I heard Emmie crying and fear like I had never experienced before gripped me. "Layla?"

"Listen to me, Jess." Her voice was suddenly very calm but that didn't help the churning in my gut. "I want you to get in a taxi, all of you. Don't drive, okay? Tell the taxi to take you to the Women's Center. Emmie's water broke. I have her in Shane's car, and I'm driving there now."

"Oh fuck!" I whispered and glanced over at Nik. He frowned at me, but I was already pulling my wallet out and tossing a bunch of bills on the table. I didn't care what I was leaving. It didn't matter anyway. Nothing mattered but getting to the Women's Center. "Is she okay?"

Another pause and I heard Layla murmuring something soothingly in the background. She was trying to keep Emmie calm. After a second, Layla was back. "She's starting to have contractions, Jesse. The baby is too big for her to deliver. You know that. Just get Nik to the hospital as quick as you can. But take a taxi. I'm serious. None of you will be sane enough to drive. You'll kill yourselves."

"Okay. Fine. Just… Just keep her safe until we get there."

"I will. I love you."

Tears were already pooling in my eyes. "I love you too. Tell Emmie…Tell her…" I couldn't get the words out.

"I will," Layla assured me, knowing what I needed to tell Emmie without me voicing the words.

I was already walking out of the restaurant, and the guys hadn't even questioned me as they followed. When we were on the sidewalk, Nik grabbed my arm. "What is it?" he demanded. There was a wildness in his eyes that I completely understood. "Tell me!"

I swallowed hard, trying not to cry. "Her water broke. Layla's taking her to the hospital right now…"

Drake stepped off the sidewalk and right into the line of traffic. The taxi driver blew his horn but Drake just opened the door and slid in the front seat while the rest of us took up the back. I told the man where we were headed and then tossed him a bunch of big bills to get us there as quickly as possible.

It was lunch time and traffic was a bitch, but the driver, either scared by the menacing way Drake glared at him or the incentive from the big tip I had already given him, got us there in record time. The car hadn't even come to a complete stop in front of the Women's Center when Nik opened the door and jumping out.

He was almost incoherent when we stopped by the information desk. I pushed him aside and told the woman why we were there. The little old woman in the pink jacket gave us a smile, obviously having dealt with scared, crazy daddies on a daily basis. She gave us directions up to labor and delivery and told us that Emmie was already being prepped, whatever that meant.

The elevator ride up to the fourth floor felt like it took forever. I thought Nik was going to start climbing the wall and was glad when the door opened. We stepped off the elevator and found a nurses' station right in front of us. Every nurse was running around

THE ROCKER THAT SAVORS ME

working fast and talking faster. I stopped by the desk. "Can anyone tell me where Ember Jameson is?" I called out.

Several heads turned in my direction. "Are you family?" A nurse demanded.

I didn't even hesitate. "She's my sister." I told the woman.

She gave me a skeptical look but nodded her head. "Down the hall. Room 403. We're prepping her for surgery."

Nik was already running down the hall before I could even turn around, Drake and Shane right behind him. He pushed a door open down the hall, and I followed them in. Emmie was lying on a little bed, an IV in one arm. There was a heart monitor on her, and I was transported for a second back to the night she had been so sick. Fear gripped me even harder, and I stood there just taking her in for a long moment.

She looked pale, her big green eyes standing out in her pretty face. Nik held her against his chest, whispering something to her, and they were both shaking. This was scary. Terrifying! I wasn't ready for this to be happening. It wasn't supposed to be like this. The doctor had sat us all down during Emmie's last appointment and explained in detail what would happen, but this wasn't it.

This was rushed. There was a doctor and three nurses trying to get Emmie ready while we stood there.

A soft hand touched my arm, and I looked down to find Layla standing there. She gave me a small smile. "It's going to be okay, Jesse," she promised me.

I wrapped my arms around her, burying my face in her hair. "Are you sure? She looks scared as hell and that is scaring the shit out of me."

Layla cupped my face in her hands. "I'm sure. She looks scared because she's in pain. She's having regular contractions, and the doctor said she was already dilated to a six when we got here. That's why everyone is rushing."

"Jesse?" Emmie's quivering voice made me raise my head. She looked so tiny in that bed.

I crossed over to her side in three big strides and wrapped her in my arms. "I love you, Jesse," she whispered in my ear, and I couldn't help but hold on tighter. "I wish you all could come into the operating room with me."

So did I. But we all knew that only one person could go in with her. Nik was already putting on the scrubs that a nurse had handed him. I brushed a kiss across the top of her head. "You're going to be fine, sweetheart. Nik will be with you."

"We're ready, Miss Jameson," the doctor said, and I reluctantly stepped back as the nurses stepped up to the bed and unlocked the wheels.

Tears poured down Emmie's face as the nurses pushed her away from me, and I felt like my heart was being ripped out as she was taken from the room.

"Love you!" she called to us, and I had to turn away so she wouldn't see my tears as they spilled from my eyes.

Layla

The past hour felt surreal. It couldn't have all happened that quickly. It just didn't seem possible. One minute I'm laughing with Emmie about all of Shane's laundry, and the next I'm driving like some Indy racer down the highway with a screaming woman in the passenger seat.

I had never been so terrified in my life as was I saw all that water pool at Emmie's feet. The way she had started screaming had nearly made me start as well, but I knew that one of us had to be calm or we were in trouble. Somehow, I had been able to call Emmie's doctor and let him know what was going on.

I had been driving ninety miles an hour when I called Jesse. Between the phone, traffic, and a crying Emmie, it was a miracle that I had gotten us to the hospital in once piece.

As soon as I had pulled up in front of the Women's Center, Emmie was rushed upstairs. I had to park Shane's car and took a second to text Lana to let her know she needed to leave school and pick up Lucy. When I got up to Labor and Delivery, they didn't want to let me back to see her. I lied and told them she was my sister. They didn't have a choice but to let me go. By then they were already prepping Emmie for her C-section. I was startled by

THE ROCKER THAT SAVORS ME

how fast the medical staff was working, but Emmie told me that she was dilating fast.

I stayed off to the side so the team could work, but I never took my eyes off of Emmie. For the first time, I saw how small she was, how tiny and fragile she could be. It scared me to see her like this. I was used to seeing the strong Emmie. The woman that didn't back down from anything or anyone.

Every few seconds, she would catch my eye, and we would hold on to each other like that. It gave her some support that I couldn't offer physically since the doctor and nurses were so busy. I was scared that if I got in the way someone would ask me to leave, and I wasn't going to chance that.

When the door opened and Nik came running in, I was beyond relieved. My fear had been that they wouldn't make it before Emmie had to be taken into surgery. I would have gladly taken his place if that had been an option, but I was relieved that Nik would get to experience this with Emmie as he should.

Drake and Shane were hot on Nik's heels, moving to the opposite side of the bed and satisfying themselves with just touching Emmie anywhere they could reach. Jesse was right behind them, and it hurt me to see how lost he looked when he saw Emmie in the hospital bed. I knew there was a deep bond there, knew that it went miles deep. Each time I saw a glimpse of that bond, I loved him more.

When the nurses wheeled Emmie away, it nearly brought me to my knees to see the tears fall from Jesse's eyes. I couldn't keep from going to him. He pulled me against him but kept his head turned away so I wouldn't see him crying. Nik was quick to follow Emmie, now dressed in scrubs so he could be with her during the C-section. It was just the four of us now, and we were all emotional wrecks.

With one arm I held Jesse. The other I offered to the brothers, and they came willingly. I hugged Shane and he put his arm on his brother's shoulder. I didn't know how long we stood there like that, the four of us holding onto each other, but it felt right. It kept us all sane while we waited.

THE ROCKER THAT SAVORS ME

Ten minutes later, a nurse escorted us to a waiting room. "Miss Jameson has already been given her epidural, and Mr. Armstrong is with her now," she explained to us. "It shouldn't be long now."

I thanked her and went back to holding onto the guys. There were plenty of chairs free. We were the only ones in the waiting room anyway, but they needed to stand, so I stood between Jesse and Drake and rubbed their backs while they stared off into space. Shane was pacing the length of the room, and I wished I had an extra hand so I could offer him the same comfort.

Slowly, the minutes ticked by on the clock on the opposite wall. The ticking was starting to eat at my nerves. Jesse was growing tenser with each passing minute. The brothers looked like they couldn't handle any more...

The waiting room door opened, and Nik stood there. There was a huge grin on his handsome face, and tears just poured from his blue eyes. My heart turned over at the sight of him. Jesse was the first to cross the room. He locked gazes with Nik, and they just stared at each other for a long moment. Their laughter made me jump because I had been so tense.

Jesse and Nik hugged, pounding each other on the back. "Congratulations, bro." Jesse's voice was choked with emotions.

"Thanks, man." He stepped back and Drake and Shane gave him the same greeting.

I couldn't help myself. I had to hug him too. He pulled me into a bear hug and swung me around. "Thank you, Layla," he whispered. "I don't know what we would ever do without you." His words made me tear up, and I tried to blink them away.

When I was on my feet, I held onto his arms. "How is she?"

He grinned. "Emmie is fine. Tired but fine. She did beautifully."

"And the baby?"

A peculiar look crossed Nik's face. "She's perfect. I have never seen anything more beautiful in my life. And big, so big! Nine pounds and fourteen ounces. No wonder Emmie has been so uncomfortable." He laughed, shaking his head. "I can't wait for you guys to meet my daughter."

THE ROCKER THAT SAVORS ME

"Dude!" Shane shook his head. "I can't believe you said that. This doesn't seem real."

But it was and two hours later, we were let into Emmie's private room. She was lying back against the pillows, a dazed look on her pale face, but in her arms she had the most precious sight I had ever laid eyes on. Emmie grinned up at us as we fought over who got to hold the baby first.

"So," Lana said as she took her turn holding the baby. She and Lucy had arrived an hour before, adding to our excited group. Somehow she had conned Drake into letting her be next to hold the baby, and I was itching to get my hands on the baby again. The feel of that little angel in my arms was the best thing in the world. "What do we call this little beauty?"

Emmie's eyes widened. "I was waiting to see her before I gave her a name. But now that I have her here, I can't decide." Tears slipped from her eyes. "I'm a horrible mother already. I can't even name my own child."

"Oh, Emmie!" we all exclaimed. I gave my friend a little squeeze. "Stop thinking such nonsense," I chided her. "You're a great mother already."

"I have a name I like," Nik spoke up. He was leaning over Lana, unable to tear his eyes off his baby girl. "Can I name her?"

Emmie's tears were quick to dry up. "Why didn't you tell me you had a name you liked?"

He shrugged, sending her a sexy smile. "I wanted to wait, like you did. But now that I see her, I think the same fits." He took the baby from Lana and brought her back over to Emmie. Gently he placed the now sleeping baby in her mother's arms. "Mia."

Emmie's face lit up. "That's perfect. I love it," she whispered. "Mia Nicole Armstrong."

Chapter 20
Layla

I couldn't lie. The weeks following Mia's birth were not all sunshine and butterflies. If anything, they were hardcore nightmares at times. I loved Mia from the moment I laid eyes on her, but damn that little bundle of joy wasn't exactly joyful at times.

Emmie had to spend nearly a week in the hospital. She had gotten out of bed too soon and popped her stitches, but Mia ended up staying just as long. She ended up having jaundice so bad that she looked like and Umpa-Lumpa she was so orange. She spent two days under a light, which had made Emmie hysterical.

When mother and daughter were finally home, things were great for the first day or so. Emmie was supposed to take it easy, no heavy lifting or being on her feet often. The baby was eating well and had gained weight already. But she was on a daytime sleep schedule after being under the bili light for so long.

By the third day Emmie was exhausted. Mia wasn't sleeping much at night, and that meant that Emmie wasn't either. Nik tried to help out as much as she would let him, but for some reason those two were arguing. Maybe it was because Emmie was going through some bad postpartum, or maybe it was because Nik had brought up the idea of getting married soon. I wasn't sure, and I wasn't about to ask. Not yet at least.

One morning when I came over to start on breakfast, I found Emmie sobbing at the kitchen sink. She had a bag of peas stuffed in her nursing bra, and her hair was a mess. I wasn't too confident that she had showered in the last few days.

"Emmie, what's wrong?" I asked, pulling her into my arms.

"I'm a horrible mother," she cried, her tears soaking my shirt, and I was sure she was wiping snot on me, not that I cared. Snot was nothing compared to the mess Mia had made on me the day before when she had had a very impressive dirty diaper. "All Mia does is cry. She would rather Nik hold her than me. She hates me."

"Oh, sweetie, Mia doesn't hate you. She loves you to pieces." I rubbed my hands up and down her back, trying to soothe my friend. "You just think she does because your emotions are all over the place." I pulled back enough to see Emmie's face. There were dark circles under her eyes. "When's the last time you slept, Em?"

"I can't remember. Maybe a few hours yesterday?"

I gripped her shoulders. "Listen to me, Emmie. You are a great mother. That little girl is lucky to have someone that loves her as much as you do. But you have got to stop trying to be so strong. Ask for help. Ask the guys. Ask me!" When she had first gotten home from the hospital, she had been determined to do it all on her own. I hadn't wanted to step on her toes, so I tried to stay out of the way, assuming that if Emmie really needed help she would speak up.

But the silly woman was far too stubborn for her own good.

Tears were pouring down Emmie's pretty face. "I need help, Layla," she sobbed. "I can't do this. I fucking suck as a mother."

"You fucking rock as a mother!" I pulled her close again. "Everyone needs help in the beginning, honey."

It took me a good half hour to calm her down enough to be able to talk her into eating something. After she had eaten, I helped her shower and then tucked her into bed. The guys were back in the studio finishing up, so they hadn't been home much during the day this week.

I took care of Mia for the rest of the day. I made sure that she was in a well lit room, and I woke her often. Thankfully, Emmie had started pumping her breast milk because I didn't want to disturb her. The one time I had checked on her, she was in a deep sleep. It was probably the first restful sleep she had since coming home from the hospital two weeks ago.

By the time Lucy was home, Emmie was still sleeping, so I put Lucy in front of the television and started on dinner for everyone. Lana came home but didn't stay. She had finals coming up the few weeks after Thanksgiving so she was studying more often than not. As long as she passed all of her exams, she was going to graduate with honors. It was her last semester of high school, and she didn't have to go back for anything except graduation.

THE ROCKER THAT SAVORS ME

Last week, she had told me she had applied for early entrance to a few colleges. I knew she was going to get in, but I had no idea how I was going to afford the schools that she deserved to go to. I refused to ask Jesse for help. He was my boyfriend, not my money train.

--

Things got better over the next week. Emmie's dark circles faded, and she wasn't as emotional as she had been. We transitioned Mia over to a nighttime sleep schedule, and she was starting to sleep longer at night. It was getting easier for Emmie, and I was beyond relieved that the old Emmie was starting to shine through again.

The guys had finally finished all the recording they needed to do. I was happy to have them all around the house again, and I loved getting to spend more time with Jesse, but I felt like something was up with him. He was acting strange, and I couldn't help but wonder if he was getting bored with me. I was too scared to ask him what was going on.

The week after Thanksgiving, I overheard Jesse and Emmie talking in her office. I was on my way to the laundry room and the door was closed, so I only heard part of their conversation. What I did hear made my heart crack.

"…Perfectly Clean said that they can have a new housekeeper here after Christmas," Emmie was saying.

"Will you be okay until then?" Jesse asked, sounding concerned.

"None of this is okay with me, Jesse. I don't want you to go…"

"Emmie, I'm not going far. You know I can't stay here. Not now."

I heard them moving around inside and rushed down the fall to the laundry room before they found me eavesdropping. I tossed the basket of clothes on top of the dryer and leaned back against the closed door. My heart was racing, my throat tight and burning with tears.

It was true. He was going to break up with me. Emmie was already looking for a new housekeeper, and Jesse was leaving. My heart clenched in a painful, way and my knees gave out. Slowly, I slid down the door hugging my knees to my chest as I silently cried. I was about to lose everything: my job, my home, my friends.

The guy that I loved…

Jesse

Things were put on hold for a few weeks after Mia came along.

I had hated to ask Emmie to help me when she had been so sick. Postpartum had been a real bitch, but I was relieved to find my old Emmie coming back to me now. For a while, the world had seemed dark because she was lost in a maze of hormonally induced black emotions. We had Layla to thank for helping Emmie find her way back, and I think I was deeper in love with her because of it.

Once Emmie was back to her old self, she started where she had left off. I didn't even have to ask her about it. She just did what she did best and made things happen. Things were moving faster than I had expected, and I was worried that I was going to be leaving Emmie out in the cold when I left.

Even though she was helping me, she didn't want me to go, even if I was just going to be a few houses away. It hurt me just as much as it hurt her, but we both knew that it was time for me to move on. A house was not meant for two families. Now that she had hers, I needed to start my own.

"You can visit me every day," I promised her with a grin. "And you know I can't go a day without seeing you, Em."

Her chin trembled but she was smiling. "I'm glad you have Layla. I like seeing you so happy, Jess."

I cocked a brow at her. "And how are you and Nik? Still arguing?"

She grimaced. "A little."

"Because you won't marry him?" Nik was chomping at the bit. He had asked her to marry him months ago, but she had said that they had to wait for the baby to arrive first. Now that Mia was here, Emmie still didn't seem ready. I wasn't sure what was holding her back. I knew that she loved Nik. I think I had known it before she had.

"I don't want to talk about it, Jesse." She stood and handed over the keys that she had gotten that morning. "It's all ready for you."

I took the keys and felt like the world was tilting on its axis. Tonight was the night. I was scared, anxious, and excited. I couldn't wait to talk to Layla. Dropping a kiss on top of Emmie's head, I left. I passed Lana and Drake in the kitchen, and without a word to either of them, I grabbed Lana and dragged her out of the house with me.

"Jesse!"

"It's set. Do you want to see it or not?" I called over my shoulder as I headed for the beach.

Lana stopped struggling and hurried to keep up with me. I had told her Thanksgiving night what I was doing and swore her to secrecy. I guess in a way I had been asking Lana for permission. Maybe I should have asked Lucy too because I was about to turn all our lives around. I had been afraid the six year old would let the cat out of the bag and ruin my surprise.

Two houses later, I was jogging up the steps to my new home. Emmie had moved heaven and earth to find me a place as close to her as possible. I had only seen it once and liked it well enough, but she was the one who had taken care of all the fine details: making the offer, getting everything sorted out, closing on the house. I wasn't sure how I managed without Emmie, and I hoped I never had to find out.

The house wasn't as big as Emmie's. Mine was only a four bedroom. The family room was huge, though, and had a beautiful view of the ocean. The kitchen had all new appliances, again thanks to Emmie. Other than the bare essentials, the house was empty because I wanted Layla to decorate our home.

"This is really happening," Lana murmured a while later after she had seen the whole house. "I mean, I knew that you were serious, but it didn't feel real until right now." She sighed. "I'm really glad that she fell for you, Jesse. As far as rockers go, you Demon's Wings guys aren't so bad."

I laughed. "I'm glad you think so, sweetheart."

She frowned. "Are you sure though? I mean…" She broke off, but I knew what was bothering her.

"I'm hoping to be your brother-in-law before long, Lana. That means that you are mine just as much as Layla's. I want you to be happy. Just pick which college you want and give all the details to Emmie. She knows what to do." When I had talked to Lana about my plans for the future, I had told her that she didn't have to worry about college. I wanted to make it happen for her.

She had gotten her acceptance letters to several colleges for early entrance. Stanford, UCLA, NYU, the list seemed endless. Lana deserved the best education I could provide for her. I just hoped she didn't destroy us all by picking NYU. I would miss her if she was all the way across the country, and I doubted that Drake would survive long with her that far away. Those two were closer than close. She was his best friend and vice versa. I could see for myself that Lana was hiding some strong emotions, but Drake was still determined that friends were all they would ever be.

"Have you decided?" She only had about a week before she had to get the ball rolling. Classes started in the middle of January and it was already December.

"I've narrowed it down." She gave me a sly grin. "Don't worry, rock star. I've got it under control. You have other things to think about. Like getting my sister to say yes."

THE ROCKER THAT SAVORS ME

Chapter 21
Layla

My heart was like a lead weight in my chest.

Leaving the laundry in the basket, I left the main house. I was glad that Lucy was riding the bus home with a friend and spending the night. I didn't have to worry about her right now. I didn't want to think about Lucy or anything else. In fact, I was sure that my brain had shut down as some kind of defense mechanism so I didn't instantly shatter into a billion pieces.

As soon as I walked in the guesthouse, I started tossing things around. If Jesse was breaking up with me, if Emmie was going to fire me, then I needed to pack. Moving on autopilot, I pulled my suitcase from the closet in the bedroom and started packing all of our clothes. I had saved a good amount of money since September. It would hold us over until I found another job.

Tears spilled from my eyes without me realizing it. I didn't want to find another job. I wanted the one where I got to be with the people I had grown to love…people who obviously didn't love me back!

Before I knew it, the big suit case was full and the closet was bare. I zipped up the case and dragged it into the living room. After placing it by the door, I headed back into the bedroom. The front door opened and Drake walked in, surprising the hell out of me.

He took one look at my damp face, saw the suitcase by the door, and went ballistic. "What the fuck are you doing?" he exploded.

I shrugged. "Packing."

"No. No way." He shook his head, making his overly long hair fall in his face. His blue gray eyes looked wild. "Where is angel?" He never called her Lana anymore. Everyone knew who he was talking about when he said angel. I guess to him she was his angel.

"I thought she was with you." They were like each other's shadow. Where one was the other was sure to follow.

"Jesse grabbed her and left. I figured she would be here." Drake glared at me. "Why are you packing, Layla? Why are you crying?"

THE ROCKER THAT SAVORS ME

"Because we are leaving." I told him and saw all the color fade from his face. It hurt me to hurt him like that, but I couldn't stay, not when I knew Jesse was about to crush me. Oh, fuck. I was already crushed. "Look, you will still see Lana anytime you want. Just because we leave doesn't mean you have to stop being friends."

"No. You aren't leaving!" he practically shouted. "I can't...You can't..." He broke off, unable to speak he was so upset.

"Drake." I took a step towards him, wanting to comfort him. Hurting him was the last thing I wanted. He had been through so much already. Finally, he had found something that made the world seem like a better place and I was going to take her away from him...

The door opened and Lana walked in. Drake saw her and nearly crumbled. "You can't go, angel!" He grabbed her hands tight. "Tell her!"

Lana looked from Drake to me then back to Drake. Seeing his pain, she pulled him into her arms. "Of course I'm not going anywhere."

He seemed to sag with relief. Somehow he made it to the couch, taking Lana with him. She landed on his lap, and he buried his face in her thick black hair. She stroked her fingers over his face, but her gaze when straight to me. "What are you doing, Layla?" she demanded quietly.

"Packing. We *are* leaving, Lana. Tonight."

"Why?" she asked, looking worried. "Why do we have to go?"

"Because Jesse doesn't want me anymore. I heard them talking today. Emmie and him. She's already finding my replacement, and I bet he is too." Scalding tears burned my face as they poured from my eyes. I scrubbed them away. "So we're leaving."

"You think that Jesse doesn't want you anymore?" Lana jumped to her feet. "Have you lost your mind? Do you not see how much he loves you?"

"I know what I heard, Lana." I turned towards the bedroom once more.

"You only think you do!" she yelled. "Go talk to him. Let him explain."

"No thank you." It was bad enough that I knew he didn't want me anymore. I wasn't going to embarrass myself by having him make excuses. "I've heard all I need to know."

"Drake, go get Jesse. Get Emmie too," Lana told him. "Tell them to hurry."

"Don't bother." I called from the bedroom doorway, but he ignored me as he practically ran from the guesthouse. I glared at my sister. "This won't change anything, Lana. We are still leaving. Make this easier on you and Drake and just help me so we can go."

She just stood there, crossing her arms over her chest. "I can't believe you would doubt how much Jesse loves you. Even for a second. God, Layla! I get sick of hearing him say it, but I never doubt him when he does."

"He hasn't been the same lately," I told her. "I can feel the emotions churning in him."

"That isn't because he has stopped loving you, idiot!"

"How the hell do you know?" I exploded. She opened her mouth to say something but I didn't want to hear it. "I'm through talking about this. I have things to do."

Behind her the door swung open. Emmie came into the living room like a little tornado. "Lana, seriously! What the hell have you done to Drake now?" she stormed. "I couldn't make sense of anything he was saying except that it was about you."

"I haven't done anything!" Lana pointed at me. "Layla's packing and apparently it's your fault. She heard you and Jesse talking earlier today."

Emmie's eyes widened. "Then why are you leaving?" she demanded. "You don't like the house? I can sell it and buy another one." She frowned. "It isn't as close, but if it's what you really want..."

"This isn't about the house," Lana informed her. "She doesn't know about the house."

Emmie threw her hands in the air. "Then please tell me what it *is* about! Because I'm at a loss here ladies."

They weren't making much sense to me. I didn't know what either one of them were talking about. "This is about you hiring another housekeeper. This is about Jesse leaving because he can't stand to be around me."

"Do you think I *want* you to leave?" Emmie put her hands on her hips, glaring at me. I couldn't help but notice that she was looking more fit and beautiful every day. "Have you lost your mind? I would give my right arm to have you stay with me forever, Layla. There has never been someone like you in my life, someone who takes care of me and put ups with me, and still loves me like you do. You are my best friend, Layla!"

"Then why are you hiring another housekeeper?" I wailed.

"Because you are going to have your own house to worry about!" she shouted at me. "You can't take care of your house and mine too."

"What house?" They kept talking about a house, and I was so confused I didn't know what to think. This whole thing was giving me a huge headache.

Jesse

I was still in the shower when I heard my door open. The glass door opened and Drake stood there, breathing hard. "Dude!"

"Layla's packing! She's going to leave," he burst out.

"What?!" I still had soap all over me but to hell with that. I pushed past my friend and grabbed a towel. I moved so fast that I nearly fell on my ass. Wet feet were slick on tile! Righting myself, I wrapped the towel around my waist and ran through the house still dripping wet.

My heart was full of dread. Why would Layla be leaving? What the hell had I missed?

The contrast of the cool evening air on my wet body was a shock to the system, but I didn't slow down as I raced over the patio and across the little yard to the guesthouse. The door was wide open. The first thing I saw was Layla's big suitcase by the door, and my heart actually stopped for a moment.

"What house?" I heard Layla ask.

THE ROCKER THAT SAVORS ME

"The house that I asked Emmie to buy for us," I told her. I crossed the room and grabbed hold of her hands. They were trembling or maybe it was mine that were trembling. "Layla, what are you doing? Why are you packing?"

Tears made her chocolate eyes glittery. "Because you don't want me anymore," she whispered, but there was doubt in her voice. "At least I thought you didn't. I-I-I heard you and Emmie talking earlier. You said you had to go."

"Of course I have to go. We all do. I want to sleep with you in my arms ever night. We can't do that here, not without confusing Lucy." I cupped her face in both my hands, wiping a few errant tears away as they slipped from her eyes. "I wanted to surprise you. Give you the house and the ring at the same time."

"Ring?" She breathed. Her eyes were huge in her beautiful face.

"This wasn't how it was supposed to happen," I muttered, reaching for the towel around my waist as it started to slip. Lana was standing by the door, and I didn't want the girl that was going to hopefully be my sister-in-law to know what I looked like naked. I glanced at her and then Emmie. "Mind giving us a minute here?"

"You and I are going to have a serious talk later, Layla!" Emmie muttered as she left. "My best friend and she thinks that I want to get rid of her…"

I sighed and waited for the door to close behind them before I gave Layla my full attention. "Now tell me what I missed. Why would you jump to such a conclusion?"

"You've been acting so off lately. Your mind is always wandering. I thought you were getting bored with me. And today when I heard you and Emmie talking I just lost it. It broke something inside of me." More tears poured from her eyes. "I love you, Jesse. If I lost you it would kill me."

"Oh, baby!" I rocked her against me. "It's the same for me. It's been like that from almost the second I heard your laugh that first day we met. I love you. I need you." Her arms wrapped around my waist, and I couldn't help the way my body responded. I was addicted to her touch, but I had things to tell her before I let my other head take over.

"Have I ruined it?" she whispered. "I didn't mean to ruin it."

"No, Layla. You haven't ruined anything. This might not be how I had planned to tell you, but you haven't messed anything up." I brushed a kiss over her eyes, tasting the salt of her tears on my tongue. "I knew that I wanted to spend the rest of my life with you after that first weekend. Emmie started making all the arrangements for me. For *us*, sweetheart. Neither one of us was happy about my moving out, but I can't start our lives together sharing a house with her and the guys. So she found us a house just two houses over."

"What?" she exclaimed. "The yellow one that just went on the market?"

I grinned. "Yeah, that's it. Do you like it?"

"It's beautiful from what I've seen of it. But…"

"No buts." I hushed her with a quick kiss. "It's ours. Four bedrooms so the girls each get their own room…and there is room enough for an addition to the family if we can fit that in later on." I hadn't really thought about having kids of my own, but after holding Mia for the first time, it had become a kind of ache in my chest. I wanted my own baby. Layla's baby.

"That…That sounds really wonderful." She smiled up at me.

I felt a dopey grin split my face. "Yes it does."

"I'm really sorry."

"I guess you won't eavesdrop anymore, huh?" I placed another quick kiss on her lips.

"Nope, never again."

"Good." I pushed her back against the wall. "Will you marry me, Layla?" I murmured, kissing a path from her ear down her neck. "Will you spend the rest of your life letting me spoil you? Letting me make you happy?"

"I can't imagine being more happy than I am right now." She shivered as I sucked on the sensitive spot where her neck and shoulder met. "But I'm willing to spend the rest of my life letting you try."

THE ROCKER THAT SAVORS ME

Epilogue

I had thought the end of that stupid tour would never get here!

I was rushing through the house making sure that everything was in order. Determined that the house was going to be just right for when Jesse got home. I hadn't seen him in two weeks—two incredibly long, agonizing weeks! It might not be a long time for some couples, but for me it was an eternity.

From the day we were married—which had taken place in at a little chapel in Vegas the day after Jesse had proposed—we hadn't spent a night apart in the two years that we have been married, not until this stupid, completely retarded tour came up. Sometimes, I hated that my husband was the big bad ass rock star that everyone was dying to see live!

Lucy came into the house, tossing her backpack on the sofa. "Is he home?" she asked excitedly. "Did I miss it?" Now eight years old, Lucy had changed quite a bit over the last two years. Her hair was kept short with little ringlets framing her beautiful face, and she had shot up a good six inches in the last year alone. Since I had married Jesse, she had blossomed even more into a young woman that I was incredibly proud of.

Jesse had been the one to bring up the topic of adoption, determined that he wanted Lucy to know exactly how much he thought of her as his. Lucy hadn't needed to be asked twice, and six months after we had gotten married, she had officially become our daughter. It had been weird at first. Lucy didn't know if she wanted to call us "Mom and Dad" or not. We had let her figure all of that out on her own. It took some time, but after a while she had slipped into calling Jesse "Dad." She and I were still figuring out if she wanted to call me "mom." From time to time, she slipped from calling me Layla to calling me Mom.

I grinned down at her as I fluffed up the pillows on the sofa. "No, baby. He hasn't gotten home yet."

"Thank goodness." She hugged me tight and flopped down on the sofa. "I didn't even want to go to school today because I was scared I wouldn't be here when Dad got home."

THE ROCKER THAT SAVORS ME

"Emmie texted me about an hour ago, so it shouldn't be too much longer," I assured her as I continued to straighten up the living room. I loved the house that we had made a home. Actually, it was as perfect as it could get, but I needed to do something to keep busy or I might lose my mind!

"I wish we could have gone with him this time." Lucy sighed. The last few times Demon's Wings had gone on their mini tours, Lucy and I had gone with them. This time it hadn't been possible because Lucy had school. Even though she was now in a private school, she couldn't be missing that much school at a time, especially with all the extra work she had from her creative writing classes her teachers had put her in.

"Me too, baby." I dropped down beside her on the sofa and pulled her close. For two weeks, it had just been me and her. No going down the beach to see Emmie and Mia whenever the mood struck. It had been kind of lonely for us, but we had gotten through it together.

To distract ourselves, I turned on the flat screen, and we settled down to watch one of Lucy's favorite shows. I tried not to glance at my phone every five minutes to check the time or see if Jesse had texted me, but my eyes were drawn to it like magnets.

The front door opening startled me, and I jumped. I heard something heavy hit the floor in the entrance hallway and then the door slammed shut. "Where are my girls?"

Lucy was already up and skipping out of the living room. I was slower to get up and by the time I reached the hallway, Lucy was already in Jesse's arms. He swung her around a few times, making her giggle. When he sat her on her feet, he pulled her close and gave her a tight hug. "Missed you, Lu," he murmured against her curly head.

"I missed you too, Dad."

I stopped a few feet away, taking in the man I loved more than life itself. He looked tired. Dark shadows under his eyes told me that he hadn't been getting much sleep since he had been gone. Neither one of us could sleep well without the other. He needed a shave; dark stubble shadowed his jaw and head. His shirt was wrinkled, and his jeans had a stain on one thigh that attested to too

THE ROCKER THAT SAVORS ME

much fast food. All in all, he was the sexiest, most heartwarming sight that I had laid eyes on. "Well I definitely missed you!" I informed him with a welcoming smile.

Jesse's bald head snapped up, and I watched in fascination as his eyes rapidly changed colors. I would never get over his eyes. Even after two years of marriage they still made me melt. Right now, they ate me up, and I had to fight the urge to drag him upstairs. "Welcome home, Jess."

With the speed of lightning, he had me in his arms. His fingers tangled in my hair and his lips devoured mine. I kissed him back, desperate for a taste of him. You would think we hadn't seen each other in years instead of mere weeks. When he finally raised his head, we were both breathless.

Jesse pressed his forehead against my own. "Yeah, this isn't going to happen again!" he muttered. "You either go with me or I'm not going."

"Agreed." I brushed a quick kiss over his lips and then took his hand and tugged him into the living room. "Are you hungry? I haven't cooked yet, but I can make you a sandwich or something."

"No, babe. I'm not hungry." He flopped down on the sofa and pulled me down beside him. Lucy took her usual place on his other side, and the television was forgotten as we made him tell us all about the tour. For more than an hour, he indulged us.

"What's been going on around here?" he asked after a while. "We've talked every day, but that doesn't mean you girls tell me everything."

I glanced over at Lucy who was eying me questioningly. She and I had been keeping something from him this last week. It wasn't exactly something that you told your husband over the phone, and I had been so anxious about it that I broke down and confided in Lucy... "What?" Jesse laughed.

I bit my lip. "There is something..." I began.

"But we wanted to tell you face to face," Lucy cut in.

"Did you two adopt another pet?" He raised a brow at Lucy. "Please tell me it's a dog and not another lizard, Lu. Or a freaking snake!"

THE ROCKER THAT SAVORS ME

Lucy had a thing for exotic animals it seemed. She had conned Drake into buying her an iguana last year for her birthday without talking to us about it. Then for Christmas Lucy had actually asked for a python. The girl was crazy about the yellow and white snake that she had named Zippy. Big, bad rock star Jesse Thornton? Not so much. He steered clear of Zippy and Lucy's room.

"No, Dad. It isn't about a pet," Lucy was quick to assure him.

"Jesse, remember before you left you said you thought it was time to start on a few additions..?" I stopped when he turned those ever changing eyes on me. "I hope you really are ready."

"Layla are you trying to tell me you're pregnant?" he demanded.

I grinned. "Maybe." We had been talking on and off about having a baby from the day we got married. It seemed like every time one of us was ready something would come up and we would put it off for a little longer. This time it had been completely taken out of our hands because I was still on the pill until I had found out that I was pregnant.

He growled and pulled me onto his lap. "Really? You are really pregnant?"

I nodded. "Yes. I saw the doctor last week when I realized I was late. I'm eight weeks pregnant." I pulled the little picture out of my back pocket where I had put it that morning. The night before Lucy and I had stared at it for hours until we had fallen asleep on mine and Jesse's bed.

"The doctor wanted to make sure how far along I was and did an ultrasound," I told him as I gave him the little glossy picture.

Jesse stared down at the almost unintelligible blob of dark swirls in wonder. After a moment, he frowned. "Where is the baby?" he finally asked.

I looked over at Lucy and we both grinned. "Well, this little black thing here is a baby," I told him, and he nodded his bald head.

"Okay. I see it now."

Lucy turned and got on her knees so that she could see the picture too. After a minute she touched her finger to the picture.

THE ROCKER THAT SAVORS ME

"And that little black thing there is another baby," she informed him.

"That's cool...Wait! What?" He turned his head from side to side. Looking at me first, then Lucy, and then back to me again. "What does she mean there is another baby?" he whispered.

I leaned forward and brushed a kiss over his slightly gaping mouth. "What she means, Big Daddy, is that we are going to have more than one new addition. It's twins, Jesse."

"Oh..." He blinked a few times, and I watched as tears gathered in his amazing eyes. "We're going to have twins," he whispered. "That's amazing."

"It sure is." I reached for the cordless phone and started dialing. It rang three times before someone answered. "Hey!" I greeted when I heard Emmie's voice. Before she could say more than two words, I interrupted her. "Can you come over? Like now? Run if you can!"

"Um...You aren't hurt or anything, are you?" She sounded concerned.

"Nope, I just really need to see you." I hadn't seen my best friend in what felt like forever. Two weeks away from people I normally got to see on an hourly basis had been brutal. And now that she was home, and I had already shared my news with Jesse, I needed to share it with Emmie or I was liable to burst.

"I'm on my way," Emmie assured me.

Jesse was still in a kind of daze staring down at the picture in his hands when the front door opened and Emmie came into the living room. Her hair was tangled around her face and Mia was hanging from her hip. Behind her was Nik, and I was just as happy to see him as I was Emmie. "Okay, I'm here!" Emmie frowned when she saw the look on Jesse's face. "What's up with Jess?"

Taking the picture from Jesse's slackened fingers, Lucy jumped up and waved the picture at Emmie. "Look! Look!"

Emmie took the picture, and her eyes grew wide as soon as she realized what she was looking at. "You're pregnant!" she exclaimed. "That's awesome." Her eyes scanned the photo, and I knew the instant she figured it all out. "Oh. My. GODS!"

Nik was laughing. "What is it, baby?" He glanced down at the ultrasound picture over her shoulder and frowned, unable to make out anything just as Jesse hadn't.

"Dude!" Jesse was back to himself. "Nik, man. I'm having twins!"

"What?!" Nik took a closer look at the picture. "Holy shit! Good job, bro!"

It was a long time later before Jesse and I had any alone time. Lucy was finally in bed and Emmie and Nik had only left a few hours hour before. I was lying on our bed in Jesse's arms, and I couldn't help but feel anything but completely and utterly happy. My eyes started to drift closed. Jesse's lovemaking had really tired me out. After so much time apart, we had a lot of loving to catch up on.

"Does Lana know?" Jesse's question made my eyes snap open. "Have you talked to her?"

I sighed. Thinking about Lana always made my heart hurt a little. "I've talked to her every day on the phone…but I haven't told her about the babies." Like with everyone else, I wanted to tell my sister in person about her becoming an aunt.

"Maybe we should visit her tomorrow." Jesse murmured.

"Okay." I snuggled closer, yawning as I closed my eyes once more.

"Layla?"

"Mm?"

"I love you." He kissed the top of my head, and I felt his breathing even out as he drifted off to sleep.

"I love you, Jesse."

THE ROCKER THAT SAVORS ME